Scarlet felt the heat of his palms caress her cheeks and then his mouth was soft on hers and he kissed her. Oh, how their mouths needed each other… It was a soft morning kiss and because of it, Scarlet knew, she would float better through the day.

She kissed him back, feeling again the lips she missed, and so gentle and unexpected was he that Scarlet felt tears sting in her eyes.

But it was just a kiss and neither pushed for more.

'Look at me,' Luke said, still holding her face, yet she would not meet his eyes.

'I can't.'

'You can…'

But she couldn't. Not after what had happened.

Dear Reader,

Luke and Scarlet surprised me all the time as I wrote their story.

Sometimes I wondered how they would get to their happy ending. This couple had so much to work through, and yet every time I doubted they could Luke stepped in and reassured me that he knew where they were headed.

I love a hero who is one step ahead—not just of the heroine but also the author!—and Luke has the calm assuredness that I felt Scarlet needed. I *do* believe in love at first sight, and their story confirmed that for me.

Happy reading!

Carol x

THE SOCIALITE'S SECRET

BY
CAROL MARINELLI

Published in Great Britain 2016
By Mills & Boon, an imprint of HarperCollins*Publishers*
1 London Bridge Street, London, SE1 9GF

© 2016 Carol Marinelli

ISBN: 978-0-263-26384-8

Printed and bound in Great Britain
by CPI Antony Rowe, Chippenham, Wiltshire

Carol Marinelli recently filled in a form asking for her job title. Thrilled to be able to put down her answer, she put 'writer'. Then it asked what Carol did for relaxation and she put down the truth—'writing'. The third question asked for her hobbies. Well, not wanting to look obsessed, she crossed the fingers on her left hand and answered 'swimming'. But, given that the chlorine in the pool does terrible things to her highlights, I'm sure you can guess the real answer…

Books by Carol Marinelli

Mills & Boon Medical Romance

London's Most Desirable Docs
Unwrapping Her Italian Doc
Playing the Playboy's Sweetheart

Bayside Hospital Heartbreakers!
Tempted by Dr Morales
The Accidental Romeo

Secrets of a Career Girl
Dr Dark and Far Too Delicious
NYC Angels: Redeeming the Playboy
200 Harley Street: Surgeon in a Tux
Baby Twins to Bind Them
Just One Night?
The Baby of Their Dreams

Visit the Author Profile page at
millsandboon.co.uk for more titles.

CHAPTER ONE

No news wasn't always good news.

It was just the tiniest of diversions from Luke Edwards's usual morning routine but, having poured a glass of grapefruit juice, Luke turned the television on and listened to the news as he got ready for work.

It was just after 5:00 a.m. on Monday.

There was the usual stuff that should make mankind weep, yet it was immediately followed by the news that Anya's Saturday night performance at the O2, the last in her sell-out world tour, had been amazing and she would be heading back to the States today. The reporter moved to the next piece of celebrity gossip—a football star's wife who was rumoured to have had buttock implants.

He changed channels and found that it was just more of the same.

Luke flicked the television off and, though he still had half an hour to kill, he was restless so he decided to head into work. He went upstairs and selected a tie, which he put in his jacket pocket. As he came back down he grabbed his keys and glanced in the mirror, wondering if he really ought to shave.

No.

His straight dark hair needed a cut too but that could wait for next week.

It was still dark outside as his garage door opened and Luke headed out into a cold and wet November morning. He drove through the practically deserted, sleepy, leafy village, where he lived, towards the heart of London. He had recently been promoted to Consultant in a busy accident and emergency department at a major teaching hospital.

People sometimes said that he was crazy to live so far out but he also had a flat at the hospital for the times when he was on call or held back at work.

Luke liked it that where he lived was between Oxford, where his family were, and London, where he worked. The very distinct separation between his work and home life suited him well. The village was friendly but not overly so. He had been living there for close to a year now and was getting to know the locals at his own pace. Luke knew that, despite what others might think, he had made the right choice.

Or not.

It all depended on today.

It was a long, slow drive but he was more than used to it. Often he listened to music or a lecture he had heard about, but this morning he turned on the radio.

He needed to know if there was any news.

For the last four days Luke had been on edge and hypervigilant while doing all he could not to show it.

The traffic was terrible, he was told.

Thanks for that, Luke thought as he glanced at the time.

There was a huge snarl-up on the M25.

Luke was in the middle of it.

Finally, just before 7:00 a.m., the sun was coming up, the hospital was in sight and a new day had dawned.

He drove towards the underground car park, where he had a spot reserved, and was just about to flick off the radio, as reception was disappearing, when there was a break in a song.

'Unconfirmed reports are starting to come in that Anya...' the newsreader said, and Luke sat, blocking the traffic and listening to the brief report, before he drove into the basement. He parked but, instead of heading straight into work, Luke sat for an essential moment to collect himself.

His instincts had been right.

Today was the day, just not for the reasons he'd hoped.

Luke got out of the car and went up the elevator and made his way through the hospital.

Security guards were starting to race towards the accident and emergency entrance but Luke refused to rush. The only concession that his skills might be immediately required was that, as he walked along the corridor, he put on his tie.

'Morning,' Luke said to Geoff, one of the security guards, as he raced past him.

Not 'good morning'.

They weren't any more.

'Have you heard who's coming in?' Geoff answered by way of response, though he did slow down and fall into step with Luke.

'I have.' Luke nodded. 'It just came on the news. Can you call for backup and start setting up the security screens? How long until she gets here?'

'Ten minutes.'

Luke nodded his thanks and walked into the department.

'Thank God you're here early.' Paul, his registrar, came straight over.

Yes, Paul was very glad that his boss was here. Luke Edwards epitomised the calm that the department would be needing today—Luke never got ruffled and simply dealt with what was. 'Anya is on her way in,' Paul explained. 'She's in full cardiac arrest. The place is going to blow.'

Luke disagreed with Paul's assessment. Yes, drama was about to hit but the place would not blow.

Not while he was in charge.

'What do we know?' Luke asked as they walked into the resuscitation area where the nursing staff were already setting up.

'Just what I told you,' Paul answered.

'Have you called for an anaesthetist?'

'The first on call is in Theatre. The second on is David. He's coming just as soon as he can but he's with a sick child on PICU,' Paul answered, as Luke started checking and labelling the drugs that Barbara, a very experienced senior nurse, was pulling up. 'I was about to see if Switch could do a ring around…'

'It's fine.' Luke shook his head before Paul could suggest otherwise. 'We'll more than manage until David gets here.'

'Do you even know who Anya is?' Paul checked, because Luke looked completely unruffled by the news of who was on their way into the department and the fact that the anaesthetist wasn't there.

'Yes.'

Oh, Luke knew.

Better than most.

Anya had been famous for forty of her fifty years of life and would, after today, be even more so.

Especially if she died.

'You'd better let the director of nursing know,' Luke said.

Paul gave a worried nod. 'I already have.'

'Good. I'll go and make sure the screens are up outside.'

As he went to go out, Heather, the director of nursing, was running down the corridor towards him.

'Do we know what she's taken?' was the first thing that Heather asked when she caught up with Luke.

'We don't know that she's taken anything.' Luke's response was tart and Heather flushed as Luke continued to speak. 'Let's just make sure that the screens are up and no cameras can get a shot of her.'

The media were already starting to gather. He could hear the sound of a helicopter hovering overhead but thankfully the ambulance bay was covered.

Right now it was about affording Anya some privacy.

Whether she would want it or not.

Paul came outside and briefed them further. 'Ambulance Control has just called. It's an unspecified drug overdose...'

'Well, that was never going to happen.' Heather's response was sarcastic.

'If you want to help—' Luke had heard enough innuendo and the patient hadn't even arrived. He turned and faced Heather and made his feelings on the subject very clear. '—then cast judgement aside. If you can't manage that—leave.'

He meant it.

Luke had long ago learnt not to judge and to keep his own feelings very much in check, and it would take everything he had in him to maintain that today.

'I was just—' Heather attempted.

'Well, please don't,' Luke interrupted.

Heather looked over at Paul and they shared a glance. Luke had worked at the Royal for just over two years now. He was never the sunniest of people but he rarely snapped and his mood seemed particularly dark today.

The ambulance arrived and as Luke opened the doors

he saw that Anya was being given cardiac massage by a paramedic and that a sun-tanned man was shouting orders in a strong Californian accent. He informed Luke, only when asked, that his name was Vince and that he was Anya's private physician.

Luke already knew.

And he hated that man more than anyone could possibly imagine.

'What's the story?' Luke asked him, as the paramedics worked skilfully on the unconscious woman while they wheeled her in and Luke pulled on a gown and gloves.

'She must have taken some sleeping tablets,' Vince said.

It was a vague response but, with time of the essence, for now Luke ignored him. Instead, he listened to Albert, one of the paramedics, who relayed far more information than the private physician seemed willing to give.

'She was found unconscious by her daughter at six a.m.,' Albert said, as they moved Anya over to the resuscitation bed.

'Semiconscious,' Vince corrected.

'The daughter, Scarlet, is hysterical,' Albert said. 'It was hard to get any information out of her. Apparently Anya was given an opiate reversal but then vomited and went into respiratory and then cardiac arrest.'

'What has she taken?' Luke asked Vince, but any clear information remained unforthcoming.

'We're not sure.'

Albert gave Luke a wide-eyed look, which he took as meaning that the paramedics had had as much trouble extracting details.

Paul took over the cardiac massage as Albert relayed the rest of what he knew. 'There were no bottles or syringes and she had been intubated before we arrived.'

Oh, so they'd had a little tidy up, Luke thought, and he

looked over to Vince as he listened to Anya's chest. 'What medication is she on?' Luke asked.

Vince gave Luke a short list that consisted of antianxiety medications and some light sleeping tablets.

'So why are there no bottles or packets to be found?' Luke pushed.

'I give Anya her medication,' Vince answered coolly. 'I also have her on a strict regime of nutrients...'

'We'll get to them later,' Luke snapped, as he started delivering vital drugs that might reverse anything Anya could have taken. 'Any opiates?'

'Only when her back injury is exacerbated.'

It would take pliers to extract any useful information from him, Luke was sure. 'Get a toxicology screen,' Luke said to Barbara, who was pulling blood as he listened to Anya's chest.

'Her chest sounds terrible.' Luke was very concerned that the tube might be somewhat blocked. 'I want to replace the tube.' He wasn't happy that the right size had been inserted or that, given Anya had vomited, the tube was clear, so he decided to reintubate her.

'Watch the vocal cords!' Vince warned.

The billion-dollar vocal cords!

Luke did not look up but Heather swallowed as she watched Luke's jaw clamp down as he was delivered an unnecessary order.

Luke did not pause in his treatment plan, he just carried on with the procedure and then secured the tube, but he offered two words in response to a very unwelcome guest in his resuscitation room.

'Get out.'

The celebrity physician did not.

Luke repeated his command, but added a couple of expletives this time, and everyone startled because Luke rarely showed emotion. He never really swore or raised his voice. He didn't need to assert himself angrily. He just chose to now.

No one present could even guess at Luke's true loathing for this man.

Luke listened to Anya's chest again and, happy that the tube was in the correct position and that her air entry was better, he pulled off his stethoscope and asked Vince to repeat whatever it was he had just mumbled.

'I'm not leaving Anya,' he said.

'Oh, but you are,' Luke responded. 'Unless you can tell me, right now, exactly what Anya has taken, and why it took so long for you to get her here, you are to leave my area now.'

Foolishly he did not.

David, the anaesthetist, arrived then and took over the care of Anya's airway. Luke called for more anti-opiate and inserted that into Anya's IV line and then awaited its effect.

'Can we can call for Security?' Luke said.

'Security?' Heather checked, knowing that they were busy outside and wondering why they might be needed in here.

'I want him out,' Luke responded, and as he did so he briefly turned to the unhelpful and unwelcome visitor in his emergency room who was diverting his concentration yet still refused to move.

Luke kicked at a silver metal trolley. It clattered into a wall and the implication was clear—Anya's private physician would be leaving by any method that Luke saw fit to use.

Paul's assessment had been right after all—the place was about to blow, only not for the reasons anyone had been expecting!

What the hell was going on with Luke?

'You make me sick!' Luke shouted, and, wisely perhaps, Vince chose to leave.

Everyone glanced at each other but Luke made no comment. He simply did all he could to focus his attention fully on Anya, who was on the very brink of death.

It was a long and lengthy resuscitation.

The drugs were reversed and her heart started beating but she had aspirated too. It was more than an hour before they had Anya under control. Then it was another fifteen minutes before she started to rouse and began gagging at the tube.

'It's okay, Anya,' Luke said, and then blew out a long breath because for a while there he hadn't thought that it would be. 'You're in hospital.'

Anya was fighting and confused, which were good signs—all her limbs were moving and her terrified eyes briefly met Luke's before David put Anya into an induced coma.

'I want her up on ICU,' David said, and looked over at Heather, who was just returning from a lengthy phone call with Admin. 'Can you call them and ask how long until they're ready and then arrange to clear the corridor?'

Heather nodded. 'I'll get onto it now. Luke, will you speak to the press?'

Luke hated how normal policy seemed to have been thrown out of the window. He was certain, quite certain, without checking, that the department would have seen several drug overdoses overnight. He just loathed how everything had changed simply because of who Anya was.

'I'll speak with Anya's family first,' Luke said in response to her request.

Even Heather had the grace to blush. 'I've put them all in the staffroom.'

'Who?' Luke checked.

'Her manager, the vocal coach, her doctor, her body-guards. Scarlet's in there too.'

'Scarlet's her daughter,' Paul added, because unless it was rugby or medicine, no doubt Luke wouldn't have a clue who she was.

'Okay, I'll speak with her now,' Luke said, as he binned his gloves and gown.

He walked out and although the department had grown busy in the hour or so that he had been working on Anya, all eyes were on Luke as he walked past. Everyone wanted to know what was going on and how Anya was.

Luke didn't stop to enlighten them.

Instead, he walked around to the staffroom and saw that Anya's huge entourage were all there on their phones. As Luke went to go in and speak with the daughter, one of them had the nerve to ask for his ID.

'It's your ID that I need here,' Luke responded, and with that line he warned them how any dealings with him would be.

'How is she?' a frantic woman asked.

'We've been waiting for more than an hour for an update,' another person said.

Luke just ignored them and walked into the very full staffroom. 'I'm Luke Edwards, I've been taking care of Anya. I'd like to speak with the immediate family.'

And there, in the midst of it all, she was.

Scarlet.

Still beautiful, Luke thought.

She was sitting, trembling, with her head in her hands. Even her cloud of black ringlets was shaking as her knees bobbed up and down. She seemed oblivious to her surroundings but then she suddenly looked up and her already pale face bleached further in recognition.

'Luke?'

'Luke Edwards,' he said, doing all he could to keep them anonymous, to not let everyone present know the agony this was. 'I've been treating your mother. Are there any other relatives?' Luke checked.

Scarlet shook her head and opened her mouth to speak but no words came out so she shook her head again but then managed two words. 'Just me.'

'Then I'd like to speak to you alone.'

'We need to know what's going on,' a woman said. 'I'm Sonia, Anya's manager.'

'I'm speaking now with her next of kin.'

Luke's stance was not one to be argued with. It wasn't just that he was tall and broad—after all, there were far more burly bodyguards than he. More it was his implacable expression and cool disdain that had the manager step back and the path cleared for him to leave.

Scarlet was seriously shaken; her legs felt as if they were made only of liquid.

She was about to be told that her mother was dead, Scarlet was quite sure of that.

'This way,' Luke said, and down another corridor they went, and when she needed him to take her arm, instead he walked on briskly.

Luke opened the door to his office and she could see his grim expression.

She was dead, Scarlet was sure.

Luke was here.

Scarlet was very used to feeling conflicted but it was immeasurable now.

She stepped into his office and the first thing that hit her was that it was so quiet.

So completely quiet and calm that after the chaos of that morning the stillness hit her like a wall.

For the first time since she had found her mother, there was, apart from her own rapid breathing, the sound of silence.

Stepping into her mother's hotel bedroom had been something she would never forget.

'Mom?'

She had crept in quietly and seen her mother lying in her bed, face down.

'Mom?'

She had tried to turn her over but Scarlet was of slight build and she hadn't been able to.

She had screamed for help and after a couple of moments a shocked butler had arrived.

From then on it had been chaos. Hotel staff had started to appear. Vince, her mother's physician, had arrived dressed, wearing trousers and a shirt, and Scarlet couldn't understand why he had taken a moment to get dressed.

She had stood back, sobbing, watching chaos unfold, and finally had picked up her cell phone and dialled the UK emergency number.

She shouldn't have rung it, she had been told.

There was already a private ambulance on the way.

Scarlet opened her mouth to ask the inevitable question—'Is she…?' But her throat had been dry and scratched from screaming and no words had come out.

Luke could see her confusion and anguish.

'Take a seat,' Luke said, and he turned the engaged light on above his door that warned people he was not to be disturbed.

Still Scarlet stood there.

She was going to hell for all that she'd done, Scarlet knew. In fact, she was going to hell twice because, instead of asking how her mother was, instead of begging

him to tell her the news, she blurted out what was now at
the forefront on her mind.

'I'm sorry...'

'Just take a seat,' Luke said.

She went to take a seat, but the chair seemed a very long
way off and Luke's hand went on her shoulder to guide her
towards his desk, but then he changed his mind.

His hand slid from the nearest shoulder to the farthest
arm and he turned her into him. Luke's arms wrapped
around her and he pulled her right into his chest and he
held her so tightly that for a moment nothing remained
but them.

There was the scent she had missed, the body she had
craved and the understanding that Scarlet had never known
till him.

It was an embrace she had been absolutely sure she
would never, ever feel again.

'I'm so, so sorry,' Scarlet wept.

'It's okay, Scarlet.' That lovely deep, calm voice hushed
her. Luke's chest was such a wonderful place to lean. To
feel his breath on her cheek and his hand stroke the back of
her hair was a solace Scarlet had never thought she might
know again. 'I think she's going to be okay,' Luke said.

He was talking about her mother.

While she was sobbing for them, for their beautiful,
painful past and all that they had lost.

CHAPTER TWO

CALM, PROFESSIONAL AND DETACHED.

That was how Luke had intended to be with Scarlet as he updated her on her mother's condition. The entire walk from the staffroom, right the way to his office, Luke had been telling himself that he was more than capable of being just that.

Luke had learnt a long time ago to push emotions aside—with patients and their relatives, with his own relatives too.

He had just never quite mastered objectivity when Scarlet was around.

It was something he knew he had better start working on.

Just not today.

Now the very last thing Scarlet needed was calm, professional and detached, but more to the point the impact of actually seeing her again meant that Luke could be none of those things.

Just yet.

As he pulled her into his arms, the embrace was as necessary for Luke as it was for Scarlet. There was so much anger and pain inside both of them. Their traumatic past was perhaps insurmountable but he dealt with the present now.

She was here. Not by the method he would have preferred—Luke had hoped Scarlet would contact him before she'd left for America today—but, yes, she was here, and so Luke held her in his arms and smelt again her hair, fighting not to kiss her salty tears away.

How messed up was that? Luke thought to himself.

He'd had a few months to prepare for the possibility of seeing her again. Since Anya's UK tour had been announced late last year, the thought that their paths might cross had been constantly on his mind. Since Anya and her entourage had touched down in England he had been wondering if Scarlet would call, if their history meant as much to Scarlet as it did to him. And, since seven this morning, when the news had broken that Anya was in an ambulance, being blue-lighted towards the Royal, he had dealt with the knowledge that he'd face Scarlet today.

Every preconceived response to her that he'd had crumbled.

Yes, there was an awful lot that needed to be discussed but Luke knew that Anya wasn't the only vulnerable, critical casualty that had been bought into his department today. Scarlet was another and, at a very personal level, he cared about her so very much more. Luke didn't want to let her go because, when he did so, back to her world Scarlet would return and so Luke took another moment to hold her.

Scarlet held him too.

She didn't just lean on him, she had slipped her hands into his jacket and wrapped her arms around his solid waist and just breathed in the delicious scent of him. Tangy, musky, male. It was a scent that she had yearned for and never forgotten and one that had been made familiar again now.

How could it be that he felt the same to her hands?

After all that had gone on, how, on this day, could Luke's arms be the ones that were holding her up?

As she was in England she had hoped that they might meet, but she had expected harsh, accusing words to be hurled at her. Words that he had every right to deliver, but instead of that he held her and made the horrible world go away for a moment.

As she had sat in the staffroom, waiting for news, Scarlet had blocked out the sounds of the people around her. Vince had been trying to speak with her, telling her what to say, insisting that her version of events wasn't quite correct. Her mother's manager, Sonia, had demanded to know where Scarlet had got to yesterday and why she hadn't been there to see her mother go on stage.

None of them knew about the row she'd had with her mother in the early hours and Scarlet had sat revisiting that as she'd done the best to block everyone else out.

And then in the midst of the madness she had heard the calm deepness of Luke's voice.

Her frantic heart seemed to have stopped beating for a second.

Oh, she had known that Luke was a doctor but she hadn't known he worked in London. When they had met he had been here for an interview but had been unsure if he'd take the job.

It had never entered her head that Luke might be here in the hospital and be the doctor fighting to save her mother's life.

Yet he was.

When Scarlet had looked up she had felt the very same jolt that had run through her the night he had walked into the club and their worlds had changed for ever.

He'd been wearing a suit that night and he was wearing one now.

It was the little things she noticed and remembered.

The other stuff was way too insurmountable for now.

And, as Luke had the first night they had met, when she clung to him he pulled back.

'Tell me.' Scarlet held him tighter, not ready to let go. If the news was bad, and given the morning's events she expected it to be, it was like this she wanted to hear it.

'She's doing better.'

Scarlet held her breath.

'Your mother briefly opened her eyes,' Luke explained. 'And she was fighting the breathing tube. That's good. For now she's been placed in an induced coma.'

'Is she going to die?' Scarlet asked.

'I don't think so but she came very close.'

'I know,' Scarlet said. 'I called an ambulance.'

'That's good.'

'You told me the number.'

She took a splinter of their time and they both examined it for a moment. A little shard of conversation that, had it come from another, would have been swept away, never to be examined again, but both now recalled that tiny memory with absolute clarity.

Scarlet looked up but not into his eyes.

Never again, Scarlet knew, would she be able to meet that deep, chocolate-brown gaze. There was just too much regret and shame for that. Instead, she looked at that lovely unshaven jaw and the deep red of his mouth that had once delivered paradise.

And Luke, feeling her eyes scan his mouth, despite the circumstance of this meeting, wanted to lower his to meet hers.

It was as simple as that.

But those days were gone and so, because he had to,

he let her go. 'Have a seat,' Luke said in his best doc-tor's voice.

Calm, professional, detached.

If he was going to do this properly then he could be no other way.

Scarlet remained standing as Luke took off his jacket, threw it onto a chair and then went around the desk and sat down, waiting for her to do the same.

'Tell me what happened.' Luke kicked the interview off.

'I told you,' Scarlet said. 'I called an ambulance. Vince had called for backup but they were taking for ever and—'

'Scarlet,' Luke interrupted, 'we need to start at the be-ginning. Before this morning when did you last see your mother?'

'Last night,' Scarlet said, and watched as Luke picked up a pen and jotted something down. 'There was a party to celebrate the end of her tour and...' Scarlet shrugged but didn't finish.

'And how was she?' Luke asked.

'I didn't make it to the party,' Scarlet said. 'I saw her back at the hotel.'

'What time was that?'

'About midnight.'

'And how was she?'

'Tired.'

'Who was the last person to see her?'

'Me,' Scarlet said. 'I think.'

'Around midnight?'

'Around one. Can you stop taking notes?' Scarlet asked. 'I can't talk to you when you're writing things down.'

'Scarlet, these details are important,' Luke said, but he did put down his pen.

He'd been using it as a distraction.

Not a word of this conversation would he ever forget.

'You found her?' Luke checked, and Scarlet gave a tense nod.

'What time was that?'

'Just before six.'

'Were the two of you sharing a room?'

'No.' Scarlet frowned.

'Were you staying in the same suite?'

'No.'

'So why were you in your mother's room at six a.m.?'

'I just went in to check on her.'

'Why?' Luke persisted.

'Because I was worried about her.'

'Why?' Luke pushed, but Scarlet did not elaborate. 'Come on, Scarlet. I can't help if you don't tell me.'

'You can't help me.'

'I'm talking about your mother!' Luke's voice rose, just a fraction. It had to if they were going to stay on track. That little pull back served to remind not just Scarlet but himself that this was work. He watched her eyes fill with tears at the slight reprimand but he had to push through. When no further information was forthcoming he chose to be direct.

'Has your mother been depressed lately?'

'No, no.' Scarlet shook her head. 'It's nothing like that. She just took too much.'

'How, when her physician keeps her pills?'

'She keeps some on her,' Scarlet said.

Luke honestly didn't know if Scarlet was covering up for her mother or simply had no idea how serious the problem was.

'Scarlet.' Luke tried to meet her gaze. 'Why did you go in to check on your mum? I'm not going to write anything down. Just tell me.'

'I was worried.'

'More so than usual?' Luke checked, and she nodded.
'I need to know why.'

'We had a row.'

'About?'

'Please don't ask, Dr Edwards.' It was Scarlet now who
rebuked him, just a little but enough for him to get what
she meant—if there were lines that could not be crossed,
if he wanted to keep this professional, then, right now, the
answer to that question could not be discussed. 'We had
an argument.'

'Okay.'

'They want my mother to be moved to another hospital,' Scarlet said.

Luke had guessed that they might. 'Well, as of now,
the only place your mother is being moved to is Intensive
Care. Here.'

'They think that she needs to be somewhere more used
to dealing with…' Scarlet stopped what she had about been
to say. Luke loathed the word 'celebrity'.

'She's in the best place and in no condition to be moved,'
Luke said. 'As her daughter, you get to make that call.'

'I don't think so.' Scarlet gave a worried shake of her
head.

'I know so,' Luke responded.

'But she has Vince. He deals with all that type of thing.'

'Yes, well, Vince is going to be a bit busy for the fore-
seeable future. After I've spoken with you, believe me,
I'm going to be speaking with him and getting a far more
accurate history than the one he gave me earlier. I may
also be speaking with the police so trust me when I say
that I'll back your call if you want your mother kept here.'

'Luke, please, don't bring the police into this.' Scarlet
started to cry and not very quietly.

He sat and watched unmoved. *Those* tears did not move

him and certainly he would not be swayed by hype and celebrity status when he made his decisions.

He just needed more facts but few were forthcoming.

His pager trilled and Luke checked it. Seeing that it was Heather, he made a phone call and rolled his eyes as she told him that the press were becoming more insistent. 'Just say no comment,' Luke responded tartly. 'How hard is it to say that?' He let out a tense breath. 'Unless there is a change in Anya's condition, or you need me for another patient, you're not to disturb me. I'm speaking with a relative now.'

He looked over and saw that in the couple of minutes it had taken to speak with Heather, Scarlet had stopped crying long enough to take out her phone. Luke watched with mounting irritation. They were speaking about her mother's near-death and yet Scarlet was checking the news reports and quickly scrolling through social media!

'What are you doing?' Luke asked.

'It's everywhere!' Scarlet said, but then she really started to cry and they weren't false tears this time. As she put the phone down on the desk, Luke saw an image, and he reached over and picked it up.

The photo that he saw was of Scarlet. She was dressed in a pair of red pyjamas and her feet were bare as she stood on the street beside the ambulance that her mother was being loaded into. Two bodyguards were restraining her from climbing in. Her black hair was a mop of wild curls, her usually pale skin was red from crying and there was a look of sheer terror on her face.

Luke looked up from Scarlet's phone and at the woman who now sat on the other side of his desk—she was the perfectly groomed star in crisis now! Scarlet was wearing tight leather leggings and a tight black top. Over that there was a large silver leather jacket that looked as if it had been thrown on at the last minute. Her black curls were now perfectly tousled. Luke knew, though, from very personal experience, that the photo was a truer portrayal of Scarlet's morning locks.

He pulled away from that memory; instead, he looked back at the phone and the image that had been captured by the press.

It showed a rare moment of reality in a very unrealistic world and this would be the photo that would dominate, Luke was sure.

Scarlet looking less than perfect.

It was the Scarlet he far preferred.

'It's going to be worse than ever now...' Scarlet could not stop crying. Yes, she was terrified for her mother, but she'd had so much hanging on today, so many plans in place. There wasn't a hope of escaping from the press now and, Scarlet knew, now more than ever her mother needed her to be near.

'They're going to make my life hell.'

'Don't feed them, then,' Luke said. Her head was in her hands, her fingers were scrunched in her hair, but she lifted her face and gave him a scornful look as he continued to speak. 'You don't have to respond to the press, just focus on your mother and yourself.'

'What would you know?' Scarlet scoffed.

'Oh, I know,' Luke said. It was pointless to sit and pretend that he could take a comprehensive history from Scarlet and leave the personal aside. 'David, the anaesthetist, will take a more thorough history once your mother has been transferred to ICU.' He handed her back her phone, and as he did so he looked at Scarlet's slender, manicured fingers and remembered hands that were as smooth as a kitten's paws.

No, anger at her spoiled, pampered life didn't now gnaw

at him; instead, it saddened him that that funny, adventurous mind had been locked away for so long.

Yes, the world was supposedly Scarlet's oyster, but Luke knew that since the day she had been born, her life had been magnified by a lens.

'You're handing me over.'

'I'm handing your mother's care over,' Luke said. 'That's normal policy when a patient is moved. I need to get back out there, Scarlet. I have patients to see.'

'What about me?'

Typical, Luke thought, but, though he tried to generate anger, though he did his best to remind himself of the spoiled princess Scarlet was and the absolute diva she could be, he failed.

'What about us?' Scarlet said.

'There's no us,' Luke lied.

He *was* angry now as he recalled all she had done, but instead of standing to leave, he sat there.

And so did she.

They sat in the silence of his office and as the world carried on outside, both went back to a time when things had seemed so different.

When hope had arrived in both their hearts.

Even if it killed them to do so, both remembered.

CHAPTER THREE

'I'VE GOT A HEADACHE.' Anya closed her eyes and massaged her temples. 'I'm going to have to go back to the hotel and see Vince.'

Scarlet frowned in concern and said all the right things to her mother but inside all she felt was relief. All she wanted was to get away from the noise of the club and close her eyes and go to sleep. It was after midnight and Scarlet had been up since seven. She had given interviews and done a shoot at London Bridge, and the rest of the day had been spent propping up her mother, telling her that she could get through the show.

'We'll get you back,' Scarlet said, and nodded to her mother's bodyguard.

'What would I do without you?' Anya asked, and Scarlet felt the knot that had lived in her chest for more than ten years now tighten a notch. And then, because she was Anya, her mother changed her mind about leaving when a young guy came over to their table with a drink and told her how amazing her performance that night had been. 'I'll just stay for one more,' Anya said.

Scarlet moved over to give the young man room to sit next to her mother but then she stood up.

She saw the exit door and started to walk towards it.

Scarlet wanted fresh air.

More than that she wanted to run.

'Hey, Scarlet...' A hand was on her arm and she turned to the face of one of her mother's bodyguards. 'I'll send Troy outside with you.'

She didn't want Troy.

Scarlet didn't want anyone, she just wanted one day, one moment to be allowed out in the world alone.

She didn't want to be here in this club.

And then she looked up and saw a man who looked as if he didn't want to be there either.

He was taller than most and, unlike others, he was wearing a suit. His hair was dark and as he raked a hand through it, it remained a touch messy. He was smart yet dishevelled, present but unimpressed, and there was something about him that had Scarlet intrigued.

'We're all leaving now,' Troy suddenly informed her. 'Your mother's ready to go.'

'I'm going to stay on.'

It was a rare request.

An almost unheard-of request, in fact, and one that did not go down too well.

'I don't need your drama now, Scarlet,' Anya hissed. 'I've been working all night and my head feels as if it's about to explode...'

'Vince will sort that out,' Scarlet said.

It ended the conversation.

Scarlet had known that it would.

Anya could stay and argue for ten minutes with her daughter or head back to Vince.

How Scarlet loathed that man!

And so, as her mother left the building, Scarlet remained.

Not alone, of course. Three bodyguards were still present, but for now at least she was minus Mom.

* * *

Luke, even before they had arrived in the club, had had enough.

It was his younger brother's twenty-first birthday and Luke really didn't want to be here, but up until now he'd had no real choice.

He'd bought dinner and had done the cursory pub crawl and had decided that he'd buy the first round here, stay for a little while and then disappear.

It wasn't a regular nightclub. Marcus's friend knew someone and had got the boisterous group into some very trendy, exclusive basement club.

At twenty-eight years of age, Luke felt old.

He'd always been more sensible than most, more responsible than most, and this place tested that to the limit. Everyone was off their heads and the noise just ate at him.

Still, it was his brother's birthday so Luke had gone along with things till now. He had been down from Oxford anyway, in London for an interview, and at lunchtime he had checked into a hotel.

His interview had been scheduled for four, which should have given him plenty of time to meet his brother and friend at seven. Except the interview had gone really well. So well that not only had he been extensively shown through the department, his potential new boss had asked him to wait back so he could meet a colleague who was in Theatre. Of course Luke had agreed. This was a senior registrar's position with a junior consultancy at the end of it at the London Royal after all.

There hadn't been time to get back to the hotel to change so he had arrived half an hour late to meet his brother and had felt on the back foot ever since. Especially here. Everyone was dressed in far less than a suit and drinking bright cocktails and were high, if not on life, just high.

'Nice to be single again?' Marcus asked, as Luke bought the drinks.

'Actually, yes,' Luke said, though it was wasted here, he thought privately.

Marcus and his friends hit the dance floor, which actually consisted of most of the place, and Luke took a mouthful of his drink and leant against the bar. He thought about the day he'd just had.

He wanted the job.

And that might prove to be a problem.

It hadn't been a difficult break up.

A painless procedure might be the best description.

Luke and Angie had been going out for a couple of years and had been about to move in together. Angie worked at the Royal and had told him about the upcoming role. But within a week of Luke applying, their relationship had finally come undone.

There just wasn't the passion that should be there for a couple who were about to move in together. Added to that was Luke's refusal to, as Angie had annoying called it, share.

Only she hadn't been talking about the last chocolate in the box!

'I know they're in there,' Angie would insist.

'What?'

'Feelings.' Angie's response had been exasperated. 'Emotions.'

'We don't all have to ride the roller-coaster, Angie. Just because I don't...' Luke had bitten his tongue rather than admit that yes, there were hurts there. Angie would have far preferred that he rise to the bait but Luke had consistently refused to. 'I guess I'm not messed up enough for a psychiatrist to date,' Luke had offered.

Luke was straight down the line and dealt with whatever life threw in his path without fuss. He saw no need for prolonged discussions as to how the past had shaped today. He had no wish to come home from a long and difficult shift and to share how it felt to lose a four-year-old or whatever agony the day had brought.

How he felt was his concern, he'd regularly told Angie. Amicably they had agreed that opposites did not attract and had quietly broken up.

There was one thing, though, that Luke needed to do if he was going to take the role at the Royal—and Luke was quite sure that it was his. He needed to be sure, very sure that Angie would be okay having her ex working at the same hospital.

Luke took out his phone and saw that there was a text from Angie, asking how the interview had gone, but it had been sent three hours ago.

It was far too late to return it now.

They were exes after all.

'Well?'

A soft voice, very close to his ear, pulled Luke out of vague introspection and he caught the heady scent of summer in the midst of winter as he turned to the sight of a young woman.

She had long, black, curly hair and huge navy eyes. Her face was incredibly pale but those large navy eyes were alert and smiling. Her lips were full and she wore dark red lipstick and not much else, just a tiny, tight, red dress.

'Well, what?' Luke asked in answer.

'Aren't you going to buy me a drink?'

'No.' Luke shook his head and tried to gauge her age. He was usually good at it but with her it was an impossible ask. Her skin was smoother than any he had seen and yet her eyes were wise. 'Are you even old enough to be drinking?' Luke checked.

'Of course I am.' Scarlet frowned at the odd question. Everyone knew how old she was. A fortnight ago she had turned twenty-three and it had been a massive affair— Anya had bought her onto the stage in Paris and had sung 'Happy Birthday' to her.

'I'm Lucy,' Scarlet said, just to test his reaction and to make sure that this man really didn't know who she was.

'I'm Luke,' he responded. 'And I'm still not going to buy you a drink.' Luke had already decided that he was going back to the hotel.

The bartender came over. 'Hey, Scarlet! Can I get you anything?'

'Scarlet?' Luke frowned and watched a small blush spread up her neck and to her cheeks. 'What happened to Lucy?'

'That's my...' Scarlet didn't finish her sentence. She didn't want to tell him about the alias that she used for hotel bookings and things. There was a heady thrill that Luke really had no idea who she was.

It was unbelievably refreshing.

'I'll have a glass of champagne,' Scarlet said to the bartender, instead of answering Luke's question.

'Put it on mine,' Luke said.

'Thank you.'

'No problem.' Luke drained the last of his drink and turned to sort out the bill. 'See you,' he said.

'You're going?'

'God, yes,' Luke said as the music pumped.

'That's not very polite! You can't buy me a drink and then leave me alone.'

Luke conceded with a small smile. 'Drink fast, then.'

She took the tiniest sip.

'And another,' Luke said, and then he started to laugh

as Lucy—or was it Scarlet?— pretended to take another tiny sip.

They were, it would seem, going to be here for a very long time.

'Who are you here with?' she asked.

'My brother and his friends,' Luke said. 'It's his twenty-first.'

'And why are you wearing a suit?' Scarlet asked, and then took another tiny, tiny sip.

'To ensure that I look like an idiot.'

'Well, I think that you look...' She looked over his body and then up to his pale face. He was clean-shaven but there was a dark shadow on his jaw, and his eyes, when she met them properly, were a very deep shade of brown. So dark that she couldn't see his pupils. 'I think you're beautiful.'

'I don't think I've been called that before,' Luke said, smiling at her Californian accent. 'Though I'm quite sure you've been called it many times.'

Now Luke looked at her properly, in the way he'd been wanting to since he had turned around to her voice.

That dress showed far too much pale skin and the red stilettos she wore looked a little too big for her skinny legs. His eyes moved to her face and she was way more than beautiful. That fluffy hair was at odds with her delicate features and her mouth was very full and red.

A little too full perhaps, Luke thought, wondering if she'd had fillers, but, God, she was surely way too young for all that sort of thing.

He wanted to kiss her.

That in itself was a rather bizarre thought for Luke. While he thought about sex for approximately fifty seconds of every minute, to want to reach over and kiss, simply kiss, a virtual stranger was something he had never felt before.

Luke checked his memory.

Nope, not once.

This was a new feeling indeed.

'So who are you here with?' he asked.

'A few people.' Scarlet shrugged but was saved from elaborating when one of his brother's friends came over. 'Hey, Doc,' he said, and picked up his drink, but then he gave Luke an odd, wide-eyed look and left them.

'Doc?' Scarlet checked.

'Doctor,' Luke said, and told her a little bit more about himself. 'Which is the reason I'm wearing a suit. I was at an interview earlier.'

'Doctor?' Scarlet frowned and, almost imperceptibly, screwed up her nose, as if he had said that he specialised in sewerage and had just dropped in for a drink midshift.

'What do you do?' Luke asked her.

Scarlet looked at the bubbles fizzing up in her still very full glass and it matched her veins because they seemed to be fizzing too with excitement. Luke really didn't know who she was, which meant she could be anything she wanted to be.

Anything at all.

But what?

And then she remembered her time in Africa and a very far-off dream, and she brought it to life but with a little slant.

'I'm an OB nurse,' Scarlet said.

'Where?' Luke asked, rather hoping it was at the Royal! 'Back in LA.'

'You'd be called a midwife here.'

'A midwife?' Scarlet checked. 'A what?'

'A midwife,' Luke said, and watched as she started to laugh.

He didn't get a chance to play with words and, oh, they

wanted to play with words, but his brother was heading over and Luke had no intention of sticking around for a drunken conversation with him. 'I've got to go,' Luke said, and as he moved to his full height from leaning against the bar he realised just how tiny she was because even though she was wearing stilettos he towered over her.

'So,' she asked, 'where are you moving on to?'

'Moving on?' Luke checked, and then realised that she was asking him what club he was off to next. 'Bed.'

'Yum!'

She took another sip of her drink and met his eyes. Luke had never met anyone like her in his life and, leaving aside the flirty offer, he actually wanted to know her some more, but well away from this dive.

'I meant…' Luke said, then gave up trying to correct her. 'Can I *Call the Midwife*?'

Clearly she didn't get his little joke because she frowned at his invitation to get in touch.

'It doesn't matter,' Luke said. She was from another part of the globe after all and, yes, he was going back to the hotel, he decided, as an overly friendly Marcus joined them.

'Can I have a word?' Marcus asked, slapping him on the shoulder.

'Sure,' Luke agreed, knowing full well that Marcus would be asking for some more money to be put behind the bar before Luke left. Marcus was studying medicine and was perpetually broke. It annoyed Luke. He himself had worked all his way through med school but he chose to say nothing tonight as it was Marcus's birthday.

But as they pulled away from Scarlet, and Luke went to get out his wallet, it turned out that Marcus had other things on his mind.

'How did you two get talking?' Marcus asked.

'What?' Luke frowned. 'Do you know her?' he checked, wondering if she was cutting one of Marcus's friend's lunch. 'Is she here with—'

'You don't know who she is, do you?' Marcus grinned. 'Do you ever come out from behind that stethoscope of yours? That's Scarlet.'

'I know that.'

'Anya's daughter.'

'Oh!'

Yes, Luke did know who Anya was. After all, she had been famous before he'd even been born, not that Luke paid much attention to such things, but he had seen Anya and her entourage leave the club. Now that he thought about it, he did recall that Anya had a daughter who went everywhere with her.

He glanced over and saw that Scarlet was trying to get away from some loud, obnoxious guy who was trying to drag her over to dance, and two burly men were moving in.

She was here with her own bodyguards, Luke realised, not the vague friends that she had alluded to. Now he understood Marcus's friend's odd look when he had come over.

Scarlet was a star.

'She seems nice.' Luke shrugged. She had. 'Anyway, I'm heading off. I'll go and settle the bar tab and put some more behind. You have a good night.'

As Luke went to the bar Scarlet came over.

'Dance?' she offered.

'I'm just leaving.'

'Just once dance,' Scarlet persisted, but he shook his head.

'Not with your bodyguards watching.'

'You know who I am now, don't you?'

'Not really,' Luke said. 'I know two of your names and

I've heard of your mother. You're not a midwife, I take it?' She shook her head and Luke glanced down at the bill he had just been given. 'There should be champagne on there,' he said to the bartender.

'It's on the house,' the bartender said, and smiled at Scarlet as it dawned on Luke that she didn't have to pay.

Scarlet's presence in the club was more than enough.

It annoyed Luke.

Not that Scarlet had been playing him along—now that he understood why, it didn't annoy him in the least—but he wanted to have bought her that drink.

'Add it,' Luke said, and handed back the bill.

'Sure.' The bartender shrugged.

He turned around and Scarlet was still there. 'Take me with you,' she said. Her arms went around his neck and Luke went to peel them off but then he heard the desperation in her voice. 'Please.' Scarlet closed her eyes. She was so tired of the noise and no doubt drama would await her when she returned to the hotel. It felt like for ever that she had been trying to escape. She looked up at Luke and he was so calm and so slightly bored with it all, as was she, and she gazed into his beautiful eyes. 'I'll make it worth your while.'

'You don't need to offer sex, Scarlet.'

'I want to spend some time with you.'

'Why don't you ask me to take you for dinner?'

'Dinner?' Scarlet frowned.

'Well, it's nearly one, so I'm not sure where.' Luke smiled but he let her hands remain around his neck and his hands moved to her hips. The urge to kiss her was back.

'I haven't eaten since breakfast,' Scarlet admitted.

It was almost that time again, Luke thought, but then he pushed that aside. Unlike most men, the thought of a one-night stand didn't thrill him—his father's perpetually roving eye meant that he'd lived with the fallout for long enough to learn from James Edwards's mistakes.

'You really want to take me for dinner?'

'I do.'

'I'm sorry I lied to you,' Scarlet said. 'I just wanted to see if you'd like me if I was normal.'

'You are normal,' Luke said.

As was his body's reaction to her.

There was a need, an absolute need to get her away from here, to just talk, to get to know her some more and, yes, to get to that mouth.

'Can you lose your bodyguards?' Luke asked. He couldn't stand the thought of them overseeing things. He wanted Scarlet away from the hype and he knew he would take good care of her. Judging by her previous offer to make it worth his while, they didn't take proper care of her either.

'I can't.' She shook her head. 'You don't get how it is—I can't go anywhere without them.'

Luke didn't play games.

Ever.

'Can you lose your bodyguards?' he asked again, and Scarlet heard the warning. If she said no, he'd be gone.

'They'll dial 911 if I disappear.'

'Well, they shan't get very far if they do,' Luke said, and he told her the UK emergency number. 'I'll take care of you but I'm not buying you dinner with an audience.'

He *wanted* to take her for dinner!

'I could go to the loo and try to...'

'Climb out of the window?' Luke scoffed at her plans. 'Why don't you simply tell them that you're having a night off?' But then he halted as he realised, for the first time, that life in her world wasn't that simple.

'Please take me for dinner,' she said.

'I'll go outside and wait down the back,' Luke offered. 'If you can't get out of the loo there will be an emergency exit. But,' he warned, 'if you tell your bodyguards what you're up to, if I even get a hint that they're around, I'll hand you back over to them. I'm not going to be playing your celebrity game, Scarlet.'

Luke meant it.

CHAPTER FOUR

WHAT THE HELL was he doing? Luke thought as he stood in a cold, dark, basement alley next to bins and looked up at the tiny windows.

She'd never get through them, Luke realised.

Maybe she had changed her mind, Luke decided, because it had surely been ten or so minutes that he had been waiting. He was just about to give in when he saw one red shoe poke out of a very small gap in a window, followed by one skinny, pale leg and then another.

'I've got you,' Luke said, as he guided her legs out and tried not to notice that her dress was bunching up. He moved his hands from her flesh and then held her by the hips and negotiated Scarlet's body out of the small opening. As he dropped her down to the ground he turned her around. She was breathless and Luke could see the exhilaration in her eyes.

Not just that she was free!

Scarlet's dress was ruched up from her rather undignified exit and she could still feel where his hands had made contact with her thighs. Now she faced Luke and, despite his very cool demeanour, Scarlet knew that he was as turned on as she was.

Her hands moved up back around his neck and she

moved into him for warmth and for confirmation of his arousal.

'Oh,' Scarlet said.

An odd remark perhaps but she could feel him on the length of her stomach and those hands on her hips let her rest there a moment. His voice when it came was a bit ragged.

'Come on.'

He got the 'Oh' comment. Luke was feeling it too.

That urge to kiss was there and a whole lot of other urges too but a stinking dark alley wasn't at the top of his wish list and her bodyguards would no doubt realise that she was missing some time very soon. So, rather than kiss her, Luke grabbed her hand and they ran up some metal stairs and out onto a seedy street and then turned into another.

Luke hailed a black cab and, a touch breathless, they both climbed in.

He gave the name of a restaurant that he knew stayed open late, which he had been to with friends a couple of times when he'd been in London. It was nice and low-key with booths where they could tuck themselves away and he could get to know her some more.

Luke wanted that.

He really did, but as the taxi took off, the driver glanced in the rear-view mirror and must have seen just who his fare was.

'Scarlet!' He turned and smiled and it annoyed Luke that Scarlet smiled back and that she and the driver started talking about Anya's performance. Was it possible to have a conversation that didn't include her mother?

'Just drop us here,' Luke said, as they reached a busier street. They walked into a different restaurant from the one he would have chosen but the reaction to her was the same there and they left.

'I told you…' Scarlet said.

It was impossible.

No, it wasn't.

Luke took off his jacket and put it around her and then he went into the pocket, took out a serviette and removed her trademark lipstick.

God, he wanted that mouth.

Luke saw a bus and pulled Scarlet onto it.

Instead of going up with the night riders, they sat downstairs for two stops.

'Someone will recognise me…' Scarlet said as they sat at the front.

'Not with my face over yours…' Luke had it all worked out.

He took her face in his hands and the shiver that went through Scarlet had nothing to do with the fact it had started to rain outside. He made her wait for first contact. She watched as he looked at her mouth and then back to her eyes and then their mouths met. She felt the first nudge of intimate flesh, a tiny precursor, a small tease, and then Scarlet found out that he *had* been holding back on her since they'd met because there was no tentativeness. He led this kiss, taking her lips between his and then parting them, only to expose bliss. It was a kiss of contrasts—his tongue was slow and tender and yet his jaw was rough and his hands kept her head steady, so there was nowhere to go but to taste and feel the bliss of Luke.

It felt like she'd never been properly kissed until now. They breathed together, their tongues mingled and probed and it took all Luke had to pull back as the bus jolted and to remember where they were.

He looked out at the dark, shiny streets and took her

hand and they stood. 'Come on…' As her hand, in his, moved up to ring the bell he halted her. 'Someone's already rung it.'

'I never have though.'

She pushed it and the driver moaned and she went to ring it again but Luke stopped her. The doors hissed open and they stepped out into the rain.

'Where are we?'

They were just a short walk from his hotel. 'We're going for that dinner I promised you!'

'And?'

'That dance we never had,' Luke said.

'And?' Scarlet asked, as she tried to keep up with his long strides, even though Luke wasn't walking particularly fast, but he halted then and turned her to face him.

'Let's see how those two go.'

He really didn't like one-night stands, they left him feeling like a user and he didn't ever want to use her.

Luke was quite sure she'd had enough of that in her life.

Not just with men.

The free drinks for the crowd she pulled, the circus that was her life.

And, perhaps more pointedly, he didn't have any condoms with him.

They walked to his hotel with his arm around her, passing through the foyer, and no one really noticed.

Without that exposed skin and red lips she didn't stand out so much and he had her pulled tight into him.

The elevator was empty and as she went to resume a kiss he pointed a finger and told her to stand back.

'Not here,' Luke said.

He was very confident and a bit bossy and she wasn't used to being refused.

'I like you,' Scarlet said, as she leant back against the elevator wall.

'Good,' Luke responded. 'I like you too.'

Up they went to his suite and as the door closed on them, for Scarlet it felt like home. It just did. There was a suit holder over the chair and an overnight bag on the bed, which was open.

She thought he'd resume their kiss now that they were alone but instead he picked up a menu.

'It's after midnight so it's just the night menu...'

'Are we eating?'

'You said that you were starving.'

'Oh.' Scarlet was very used to being starving.

She was starving all the time, in fact.

He handed her the menu and Scarlet instantly knew what she wanted. She usually stayed away from carbs but this was her night, her great escape. 'I want the club sandwich.' Then she changed her mind. 'Maybe the burger.'

She couldn't choose.

'Both,' Scarlet said, and Luke smiled and picked up the phone and placed their order. 'Twenty minutes.'

'Whatever will we do?' Scarlet smiled and Luke watched as lifted the hem of her dress and went to peel it off.

'Scarlet...' He stopped her. 'I hope we're going to take more than twenty minutes and I don't want interruptions.' Luke watched as she went over to the bed and lay back, sulking. 'They said that we should order breakfast now if we want it delivered in the morning.' He picked up the menu cards that would need to be hung outside the door. 'What?' he said when he saw that she was staring.

'I want a kiss.'

'Let's sort this out first. Tomato, pineapple or grapefruit juice...'

'Grapefruit.' Scarlet sighed, and he pulled a face. 'Don't you like it?'

'Too sharp,' Luke said, and he ticked pineapple for himself.

'Don't you like me?'

'Why do you ask that?' Luke asked. 'I don't need you on your knees within the hour to like you, Scarlet.'

He guessed she wasn't very used to that.

And he did like her and want her.

But it was more than that...

She picked up a wad of paper that was beside his overnight bag. 'What's this?'

'Just notes I made for my interview.'

'Were you nervous?'

'No,' Luke said, and then glanced up to see she was really reading his notes.

'What was it like?'

'It was an interview.' Luke shrugged but then thought about it and realised that, unless it was for the media, Scarlet wouldn't know so he amended his earlier response. 'I wasn't nervous because I was quite sure I wouldn't get the role. Now I am nervous because I want it.'

'Do you think you'll get it?'

'I think so.'

'So why be nervous?'

Luke usually left such conversations where he had first left this one—at a shrug. There was no point discussing it till he knew if the role was his, but Scarlet was curious rather than nosy and he forgot about breakfast for a moment and, to his own surprise, told her something that was on his mind.

'My ex works there,' Luke said. 'We only broke up last month. I need to speak to her about it.'

'Why?' Scarlet asked. 'Do you still fancy her?'

'No.'

'Does she still fancy you?'

'No.' Luke smiled. 'It was a long overdue break up.'

'No problem, then.' It was Scarlet who shrugged this time. 'I don't believe you, though.'

'Sorry?'

'Can you ever unfancy someone?'

'Actually, yes.' Right up to the moment the words left his mouth Luke had believed it, but in that split second he disbelieved it also.

Not when he looked at Scarlet, who had just kicked off her shoes and was still reading through his notes. Her knees were up and she rested on the pillow, holding the paper above her face, rather than sitting up to read. He could see the hollow of her stomach and the jut of her nipples through her dress and then she moved the papers so that she could see him and smiled.

And Luke doubted if he could, as Scarlet put it, ever unfancy her.

'Breakfast,' Luke said, and tried to take care of the morning.

'I don't eat breakfast,' Scarlet said. 'Just a coffee.'

And again, for Luke, everything changed. He wanted dinner over and done with, he wanted to dance, and then he wanted her naked and writhing in the bed.

'You're going to be starving in the morning, Scarlet,' Luke said.

Something in his voice had her throat tighten and she put down the paperwork.

'Then you'd better read me the menu.'

'Cereal, muesli?'

'Muesli.'

'Full cream or—'

'Full cream, I think,' Scarlet interrupted. 'Don't you?'

With each tick they got sexier.

'Toast?' He looked at Scarlet and she shook her head.

'Too many crumbs.'

She came over and stood in front of him and they read it together.

'Ooh, bacon,' Scarlet said. 'That's very forbidden.'

Hurry with that dinner, Luke thought, because he was pressing her bottom into him and his face was in her hair and he wanted to turn her around and have her against the wall.

And she wanted him so badly, in a way she never had. His hand pressed onto her stomach and now his mouth was on her neck and his kiss to her skin was so sexy and gentle.

'I was watching you from the moment you came in,' Scarlet said.

Luke turned her around and looked down at her. 'I wanted you from the moment I turned around.'

There was a knock at the door. He was tempted, so tempted to ignore it, to call to leave it outside, but, no, they should have dinner.

As the trolley was brought in, Scarlet turned on the television and found a music channel.

Luke paid the tip and as soon as the door closed they faced each other. Luke took off his shirt.

Then his shoes. And she watched as he stripped.

What a body.

Muscular, lean and very, very male, given she was used to men more waxed and bald than even she was.

'You have hairy legs.' Scarlet smiled.

'I wouldn't make it off the rugby field alive if I didn't.'

Scarlet peeled off her dress in one easy motion and Luke made no moved to stop her as she took off her tiny knickers and took her seat at the little table.

The burger was fantastic.

Fat, juicy, and when some onion fell on her breast, Luke kindly retrieved it for her with his fingers and they fed each other dinner.

It was the most amazing meal she had ever had because it came from his fingers.

He'd be laughed off the rugby field if they could see him because Scarlet was bringing food to his mouth and he didn't just suck on her fingers, he kissed her palm deeply. When the meal was over, Luke stood.

'Dance?' he said.

With just her shoes on, Scarlet stood.

She went into his arms and he pulled her right in.

Scarlet felt that chest naked against her cheek and her hands moved around his waist; she had never been any-where nicer in the world. Luke felt her sway against him and inhaled the scent of her hair and then lifted her face so he could again meet her lips, and then they danced like no one was watching.

CHAPTER FIVE

THAT WAS THEN.

And here they were now, sitting in his office, trapped in the fallout of that time.

It was too painful to think about that night with the other there in the room. Or rather it would be impossible to think about what had taken place in the morning and hope to hold a sensible conversation.

And sense was the one thing that he had to maintain today.

'I don't know what to do,' Scarlet said, though the words were said more to herself than to Luke.

Her head was back in her hands as she sat at his desk crying, not for effect, just because she honestly didn't know what to do.

She'd had plans.

Big ones.

She had told her mother some of them.

And now this had happened.

Luke looked again at the picture of her getting into the ambulance and pushed aside the anger he felt. Scarlet had found her mother unconscious and close to death after all.

For all her money and fame she couldn't buy the one thing she required most now. More than ever before, Scarlet not only needed space and peace, she deserved it.

'Why don't you go somewhere else and check in under Lucy…?' She had told him about that secret name when they had fed each other dinner and he had found out more about her life.

How her mother's fame had been declining but then Scarlet had been born and the beautiful baby Anya had worn on her hip had shot her back into stardom.

He had gleaned that Scarlet had been nothing more than a pretty accessory to wear along with her mother's designer gowns and had been far too precious to send to school.

Luke hadn't said that to her at the time, of course. Whatever he felt, he rarely shared.

'Check in under your alias,' Luke suggested.

'And that will buy me a couple of hours before someone tips them off,' Scarlet said. 'And what happens when I want to visit my mom? The press are everywhere, they'll be all over me.'

'Only because you'll arrive at the hospital with your bodyguards in tow,' Luke said. 'You could dress down and come in through the maternity entrance. Nobody would even know that you'd arrived. Security could take you straight up to ICU without anyone noticing. Visiting your mother doesn't have to be a big deal.'

Scarlet just couldn't buy it. 'I need the security now more than ever. The press are more interested these days in me than…' Scarlet stopped speaking then.

She couldn't tell anyone about the jealous row that she'd had with her mother last night.

'Luke, can you help me, please? I need to get away, I need space, peace.'

'We tried that once, remember?' Luke reminded her. 'And you blew it.'

'I won't this time.'

'I don't believe you, Scarlet.' Luke shook his head. 'I

actually don't think you can help yourself. You crave attention...' Luke halted. He didn't want to add to her distress but, two years on, he was still hurting and angry and it was proving hard not to show it.

'I know that it might be a disruption for you if I came to stay...' Scarlet persisted, but Luke swiftly broke in.

'A friend coming to stay shouldn't be a disruption. It's only when that friend brings an entourage along...' He was struggling to hold on to his temper.

'Or is it because your partner wouldn't like it?'

Luke didn't respond. He didn't say he didn't have a partner, that really since two years ago every attempt at a relationship had ended not just because he was cold, arrogant and obsessed with work, but for another reason— guilt. He still thought about their one night together and since then nothing had matched up.

She took his silence the wrong way—that, unlike her, Luke had moved on with his life.

Scarlet stood. 'Can I see my mother?'

'Of course,' Luke said. 'We're just preparing to move her up to Intensive Care.'

'I'd better tell Sonia first.'

'Just have some time with your mother.' He reached for the phone and asked to be put through to the head of security, and Scarlet watched and listened.

'Hi, Geoff. How is it going with clearing the corridor?'

Whatever Geoff said, Luke rolled his eyes.

'I'm going to bring Anya's daughter to see her. Can you please have all her entourage move inside the staffroom and close the door? Tell them Scarlet will be in to speak with them when she's ready to.'

Luke spoke about logistics as she dug one hand into her pocket and her fingers closed on a stone she had picked up on a faraway beach yesterday.

Oh, Scarlet had made plans. She thought about the little cottage she had found, the month she had planned where she might sort out her head space. There was no chance of that now, with her mother's life hanging in the balance.

Luke was right, though not in the way he had meant—she couldn't help herself.

He did his best to prepare her for what she was about to see but he knew that nothing really could.

They walked out of his office and a security guard stood outside the staffroom and gave Luke a nod.

'Thanks, Geoff.'

They walked down the corridor and through the department, past all the nudges and stares. Only Luke noticed them. Scarlet felt sick.

Luke parted the curtains. 'This is Barbara,' Luke said. 'And the anaesthetist, David. And this is Paul, he's a registrar...'

Scarlet didn't hear much else. All she could see was her mother's deathly white face and all the tubes, and all she knew was that this was her fault.

After all, she knew what she had said to her mother last night.

'Can she hear me?' Scarlet turned anguished eyes to the nurse.

'We don't know,' Barbara said. 'Try talking to her.'

Barbara put her arm around Scarlet's waist and Luke was relieved to step back as Barbara did the job she was very good at.

She answered all Scarlet's questions about the machines and why Anya's face was so swollen.

Luke stepped outside.

Scarlet wasn't his problem. If Anya hadn't done what she had, he wouldn't have even seen Scarlet.

He glanced at the time.

She'd have been on her way back to the States by now.

Then, through the curtain, he heard her voice and it tore at his heart.

'I'm sorry, Mom. I should never have said what I did...'

Luke took a breath to the sound of Scarlet completely breaking down and, after a couple of moments spent trying and failing to resist reaching out to her anguish, he stepped back in.

'Paul, could you please go and speak with her manager?' Luke said. 'Give as little information as you can. Just let them know that her condition is critical but stable.'

'They'll want to know more than that.'

'Of course they will,' Luke said. 'And if we let them, the press would be in here, taking photos.'

'Scarlet,' Luke went on, 'can I speak with you outside?'

He nodded to Barbara and David and then he took Scarlet into one of the relative interview rooms.

'Scarlet,' Luke asked, 'what happened last night?'

She couldn't tell him.

'We need to know if this was an accidental overdose or deliberate.'

'It was an accident.'

It had to be, Scarlet thought.

Please, let it be.

'You can tell me.'

She couldn't look at him; she wanted so badly to meet his eyes but she couldn't.

'Tell me,' Luke pushed gently. 'You said you had a row.'

She nodded.

'A big one?'

'I shouldn't have said what I did.'

'Which was?'

Scarlet shook her head. She was scared to go there, especially with Luke.

'Tell me.'

'I said that I wasn't going back to LA with her.'

'Okay.'

He held her hands then and she looked at his lovely long fingers entwined around hers. 'I said some terrible things.'

'Tell me.'

'I can't.'

'You can.'

'I said she was jealous of me…I said…' Scarlet stopped but then she made herself say it. 'I said something about our baby.'

Silence stretched as she voiced it.

Not all of it.

Just the part that rendered them lost or, worse, unsalvageable.

Wreckage that lay too deep for rescue.

It was surely time to pack up the equipment and head for home.

He sat silent for a moment and then dropped her hands and Scarlet sat staring at the floor as Luke got up and walked out.

She had guessed he would.

For two years every day had hurt but some days hurt more than others and that was today.

Scarlet sat in a room where she guessed people found out their loved ones had died and mourned her baby so badly, even if she didn't deserve to.

She had signed the consent form after all—crying and shaking, unlike Vince who had calmly handed her the pen.

It had been the worst day of her life.

Even with her mother lying near death, it still was.

But on that day there had been one saving grace—

a nurse who had sat with her afterwards and let Scarlet speak.

There could be no saving grace today.

She didn't look up as the door opened and Luke came back in.

'You've got two choices,' Luke said, and Scarlet blinked. She'd never had even one. 'I've got a flat here at the hospital you can stay in for a few days, but on several conditions.'

She stared up at his chin again. 'I can stay?'

'As long as you agree to my conditions.'

'Which are?'

'You lose the phone.'

'I need to know how my mother is—'

'I work here,' Luke interrupted. 'I'll be kept updated.'

'But I need to see her, to be with her.'

'She is in a coma,' Luke said. 'There will be plenty people keeping a vigil, I'm sure. I think right now you need some time to take care of yourself.'

'What are the other conditions?'

'This time you don't tell your bodyguards where you are.'

'How?'

His face darkened but, instead of stating the obvious—that she simply didn't tell them—he threw her blue theatre scrubs and a theatre cap, and wrapped up in them were some clogs.

'I'll give you directions...' But even as he said it, Luke knew it was hopeless. In the flat across the hall from him was one of the radiologists known for gossip. There were the domestics who came in and serviced it. So he told her the other choice. 'Or you can go to my home. It will be easier to keep things under wraps there.'

'Your home?'

'It's about an hour's drive from here,' Luke said.

'I can't leave her.'

'That's up to you. But if you do decide to go there, I mean it, Scarlet, if you call in the entourage, there'll be no time to give your excuses because I won't be listening. You'll be out.'

'Why do you hate them so much?'

'How do they protect you, Scarlet?'

'They keep the public back.'

'But when you wanted to make it worth my while when we met, they were fine with that?' Luke checked. 'A quick blow job and they look away?' He watched her cheeks go red. 'That's not protecting you, Scarlet. I can do all that.'

'What if something happens to her and I'm an hour away?' Scarlet asked. 'What if she dies?'

'Then I'll come home and tell you myself.' Luke didn't sugar-coat it and she sat there, absorbing his words.

She would want to hear it from him, Scarlet knew that much.

'You'll take me there?' Scarlet asked.

'No. I have to work. My car is in the underground car park. You go out of here and turn right and then follow the sign for the staff car park. I have a navy Audi. If you press the keys the lights will flash but you'll see it just as you come out the elevator. Can you drive?' Luke asked, but then checked himself. He knew the answer to that one— not very well, given all the little well-publicised prangs she'd had.

Scarlet nodded.

'On the opposite side of the road?' he checked.

Scarlet nodded again.

'What will you do for a car?'

'There are taxis.' He did the best not to sarcastically

remind her of the last time they had got into one. 'I've got friends who can give me a lift too...'

It all sounded alien to her, Luke knew, but she either wanted the real world or she didn't. He wasn't going to handle her with kid gloves, he was way past all that.

'If I need to speak to you I'll ring three times and hang up. Pick up the phone the next time it rings.'

'Can't I call you? Can I page you?'

'No.' Luke shook his head. 'If I'm busy one of the nurses often answers my page. I'll call if I have to but, Scarlet, if I get even a sniff of your bodyguards, or the press find out where you are and it's your doing, you will be on your own.'

'But people will be looking for me.'

'Write a text now, explaining you're safe but you just need some time, and I'll hit Send once I know you're safely gone.'

'What about seeing my mother?'

'We can work out those details later. Right now I need to get back to work.' He handed her one of the large yellow garbage bags. 'Leave your clothes and phone in this.'

'I'll need my clothes to change into when I get there.'

'You'll stand out like a sore thumb where I live, wearing that.'

'Luke, I don't know.'

'Then decide. Go back out there and be with your people or you hit the sat-nav in my car and press Home. It's up to you.'

He refused to make decisions for others unless he was paid to.

'Will you be okay with me being in your home?' Scarlet asked.

Luke chose not to answer that. He was about to; he could

almost feel the sneer of his lips as he went to ask when she had ever taken his feelings into any equation.

But today wasn't the day to row, he told himself.

'It's up to you,' Luke said again. 'You need to speak with David before you leave, though,' he added.

'And tell him what?'

'That you're staying with a friend.' He wrote down his home number and handed it to her. 'Tell him if he needs to reach you to leave a message on the answering machine and that you'll call straight back.'

And then Luke was gone.

David was thorough, going through all that Luke had and more.

'We'll talk again once I've got her settled into ICU,' he said.

'I shan't be here.'

Scarlet met David's solemn gaze.

'I'm going to be staying with a friend.' She waited for him to chide her.

'I think that's wise,' David said. 'Can I have contact details in case of an emergency?'

'Don't let—'

'I shan't.' David nodded and Scarlet handed him the phone number that Luke had given her.

'If you leave a message, I'll call straight back.'

'Of course.'

He left her then and once alone she took off her silver jacket and her leggings and top and her shoes and then slipped on the scrubs and the disgusting clogs Luke had brought her.

Her hair she tucked into a hat.

With shaking hands she wrote a text to her bodyguard but didn't hit Send and then she threw her phone in the bag.

But then she retrieved it.

She needed it. Her mother was desperately ill after all but, recalling his rules and knowing Luke always meant what he said, Scarlet threw it back in the yellow bag.

She walked out and followed his directions and it was slightly dizzying that no one really gave her a second glance.

Past the canteen she went and then she saw a sign for Maternity and beneath that an arrow that pointed to the staff car park elevator.

She stood beside a blonde woman, waited for the doors to open and then stepped in.

'Hi...' The blonde woman nodded to her in the elevator and Scarlet nodded back.

'Are you new?'

'I just started,' Scarlet said.

'Where?'

'I'm an OB...a midwife,' Scarlet replied.

She wished that she was. How she wished this was where she worked and that she had just come from meeting Luke.

Oh, she wanted that to be her life so very, very much.

The woman was waiting for her to give her name, Scarlet knew. 'I'm Lucy.'

'Angie.' She returned her name with a tight smile. 'You're supposed to always wear your ID, Lucy...?'

Scarlet could hear the question mark and the woman's demand for her full name and more information. 'Lucy Edwards.' Scarlet borrowed Luke's surname and gave Angie another smile and then almost folded in relief as the elevator door opened.

She pressed the key and a very dirty navy Audi flashed its lights. Scarlet went to the wrong side of the car, of course, but then remembered and walked to the other side.

She was sweating and breathless, as if she'd been running, and that damn woman was watching her, Scarlet knew. She climbed in, turned on the engine and reversed out, and as she did so she glanced up and saw that Angie was *still* watching.

Angie thought she was an impostor, Scarlet was sure. She just hoped that she didn't call Security.

Any minute now the call that she was missing would go out, Scarlet knew.

And Luke knew it too.

It was already starting.

Scarlet had been gone for too long. Her bodyguards were walking down corridors and knocking on doors. Luke went into the interview room, picked up the yellow bio-hazard bag and walked through the department into his office. He turned on the engaged sign.

Luke opened the bag and took out her phone.

I've gone away with friends for a few days. I just need to get my head around things. Don't look for me.

Luke hit Send.

'I'm busy,' Luke called, when there was a knock at his door.

'It's Angie.'

Luke frowned. Angie rarely stopped by and she was the last person he knew to ignore an engaged sign.

He opened the door. 'What do you want?'

'Are you with someone?'

'No.'

'Then can I come in?'

Luke nodded.

They still got on.

Both had agreed they would never have worked and were now colleagues and very good friends.

'What the hell are you up to, Luke?'

'Nothing.'

'So should I call Security, then? Because a certain famous woman is pretending to be a midwife and driving your car.'

'Angie…'

'What the hell are you doing, getting involved with her again, Luke?'

A few weeks after they had broken up, Angie had seen the change in him and, knowing how lukewarm Luke had been about the break up, she'd been astute enough to know it hadn't been about her. Luke had always been a bit aloof but he was frantic now and had finally told her why.

Angie had held her tongue when she'd heard that he'd had a one-night stand.

That wasn't the Luke she'd known.

And then to find out that the said one-night stand was in LA and pregnant with his child had had her even more confused.

'Are you sure it's yours?'

Luke had always been so-o-o-o careful, it had made no sense.

'Very sure.'

And in the end, reluctantly he had told her, not just about that night but some of the things that had happened afterwards.

'She's trouble,' Angie now pointed out. 'She messed with your head big-time.'

'No,' Luke corrected. 'Scarlet's lifestyle messed with my head. When I was with her she actually cleared it. Anyway, I don't need you with your psychiatrist's hat on.'

'Luke, she had an abortion without even telling you.'

'Do you think I don't know that?' Luke's response was terse.

'Just be careful,' Angie warned.

'Oh, I intend to be.'

CHAPTER SIX

SCARLET COULD BREATHE.

For the first time in the longest time, as the garage door closed behind her, Scarlet sat in Luke's car and dragged in a long breath.

Apart from having taken a couple of bricks out of a very low wall as she had negotiated the narrow driveway to his home, the drive had been an easy one.

She had kept glancing in the mirror, checking that no one was behind. At first she had listened to the radio, but when they hadn't been talking about her mother they had been playing her songs. It had been too much for Scarlet so she had turned it off.

She'd made it, Scarlet thought as she got out of the car.

The garage was small and there was a door that she pushed open, stepping into a utility room and then walking through to the kitchen.

The kitchen was far smaller than any that she was used to.

Scarlet opened the fridge and there wasn't much in there—a loaf of bread, some eggs and bacon. Scarlet thought of the lovely breakfast they had been about to have two years ago but never had.

She couldn't think about that now so she quickly closed the fridge door and sat at the kitchen table, but all she could see was her mother and those awful words from the fight they'd had replaying in her head.

Scarlet was sorry, but not for what she had said but the way those words had been delivered and the effect they had had.

But she had meant them.

It felt odd to be here.

An unwelcome guest.

She walked down the hallway and looked at the phone, and saw that the answering machine was flashing. She hit Play.

'Hi, Luke, it's Emma. Just reminding you about Wednesday.'

Scarlet swallowed. Of course he had a life.

She held her breath as the next message played but it was some man called Trefor to say that training had been moved.

Yes, Luke had a life.

Still, there were no messages for her and that was a good thing so she moved through to the lounge.

There was an open fire and some logs beside it but building a fire wasn't exactly her forte so Scarlet sat shivering on the sofa, still dressed in theatre scrubs. She just stared at the wall and wondered whether, if it hadn't been for her mother, she would have ever seen this place.

Of course not.

He was a very decent man and he was helping her out, that was all.

Even though she was sure he would rather not have had to.

Dusk arrived and apart from a trip to his downstairs bathroom she didn't move, but then Scarlet realised just how hungry she was.

She hadn't eaten all day.

In fact, she'd had nothing since breakfast yesterday.

Yesterday she had driven for miles in a car the hotel had provided, planning her escape, too busy and excited for all that was to come to stop and eat.

There had been a welcome basket at the cottage when she had arrived and in there had been some snacks and local cheese and condiments, but she had been too nervous to do anything other than put them in the fridge.

Scarlet thought about the long walk on a pebbly beach that she had taken and the plans she had started to make that could never happen now.

Anya had made very sure of that.

She wanted the stone she had collected but it was in her jacket back at the hospital.

Scarlet turned on the television and it went straight to the news. Of course her mother was at the top of the hour but, sure enough, they flashed the image of a terrified Scarlet as often as they could.

'Scarlet is holding a vigil at her mother's bedside,' the press release said. *'At this difficult time she asks for your prayers.'*

Scarlet flicked off the news and wandered into the kitchen. She opened the fridge and took out a carton of eggs but then she saw a bottle of grapefruit juice in the door.

It was almost as if it had been left there for her. Scarlet knew, from their one night together, that Luke didn't like it—he had screwed up his face and told her it was too sharp.

The memory of an uncomplicated them made her smile and Scarlet poured a long drink and scrambled some eggs, even if that hadn't been her intention when she had first cracked them.

They were lovely, apart from the bits of shell that she had to crunch through.

Maybe her mother had been right when she'd said last night that Scarlet could never survive without her.

Now, as darkness came, she was ready to check out the house.

The lounge she knew, she'd been in there for a few hours after all, so she pushed open a door and saw a study. There were shelves and shelves of books and on closer examination she saw they were textbooks.

Scarlet pulled one down and opened it at a random page and, rather than being repulsed at the image she saw, it was actually quite fascinating. Still, she didn't have time to read about ligature marks and entrance and exit wounds from bullets so she closed the heavy book and put it back on the shelf.

It was a very masculine house, Scarlet thought as she headed up the stairs. There were no unnecessary pictures or flowers but she'd love to see it in spring, with a huge vase of something pretty in the hallway.

He must have been in the middle of decorating because there were ladders and tins of paint at the top of the stairs. Scarlet found the bathroom but didn't go in. Instead, she went down the hall and pushed open a door and guessed that this was supposed to be her bedroom tonight.

She didn't go in there either. Instead, she hurriedly closed the door and headed back down the hall and into Luke's bedroom.

There were dark green sheets on the bed topped by a dark green duvet, and the bed was all rumpled and unmade. It was a very low bed with low tables at either side. There was a phone on one and some books so she knew that was his side of the bed.

Yes, she was nosy.

Scarlet opened up his bedside drawer and there were some foreign banknotes and cash and a few tickets, and she felt her lips purse when she saw an open packet of condoms, with its contents spilling out.

She counted them.

Scarlet couldn't help herself.

Oh, so he used them now.

Bitterness, anger, jealousy all rose in her chest but she swallowed them down. It was very hard to be bitter about the memory of the love they had made.

It was any woman who had come after her that had Scarlet drop the condoms back into the drawer and slam it closed.

What did she expect? Scarlet asked herself.

That two years on he'd be as stagnant in his life as she was?

Oh, but it hurt, it really, really hurt, the thought of him with another woman.

She left his bedroom and headed back to the one that was presumably hers.

And that hurt even more.

It was why she had so quickly shut the door on it but Scarlet opened it now.

Would this have been their baby's room? she wondered, then answered her own question with the very next thought.

Of course not.

Scarlet would have had her baby back in LA and the baby would have been balanced on her hip and paraded for the cameras and dragged everywhere, just as her mother had done with her.

Luke would never have allowed it, though, and her mother had told her only too clearly the impossible odds she faced if she dared to leave.

'A one-night stand?' Anya had rammed it home again and again.

'It was more than that!'

'Oh, so you're going to be a doctor's wife!' Her mother had gone into peals of laughter and her manager, Sonia, had followed suit. 'I know I told you to dream big, but please...'

Now she stood in the door way and it felt as if her arms were being pulled in two direction as her body was torn apart.

Scarlet had cried so much today that she been quite sure that there were no tears left.

For a moment there were none.

Just a scream of rage that came out so loud and so raw that it had her sinking to her knees on the spare bedroom floor and she sobbed for her baby and, yes, she was going to hell. Not just for the terrible things she had done but right now, right this very minute, Scarlet wished that her mother was dead.

CHAPTER SEVEN

'LUKE?'

It was close to ten and he just wanted home. It had been one of those days that never ended but just as he went to leave, Mary, the night charge nurse, called him back.

'I hate to ask...'

Mary did hate to ask, she could see how exhausted Luke was, but she also knew that he would prefer that she did.

'There's currently a two-hour wait but I've got a man here whose son is on ICU and all he needs is a sleeping tablet.'

Luke nodded.

'And a couple of headache tablets,' Mary added. 'His blood pressure's high and if I get Sahin...'

Sahin, the registrar on tonight, was thorough, extremely so, and he would run a battery of tests, Luke knew.

'Where is he?' Luke asked.

'I put him down in the interview room. If you need a cubicle, I can bring him into one.'

'The interview room is fine.'

Luke knocked on the door and went in. He saw a gentleman pacing and he introduced himself.

Evan Jones was doing everything he could to hold it together, Luke could tell.

'My son's not well.'

'I heard,' Luke said. 'I'm very sorry.'

'We just had some very bad news. The sister in charge suggested that I come down here. I haven't slept for a couple of nights. I really don't want to sleep...'

'You *have* to sleep,' Luke said.

No one really knew why, just that you did, and if you didn't, well, here was living proof that sleep was necessary. Evan's anxiety was through the roof and his blood pressure was high, as was his heart rate.

'Please, don't start suggesting I need to lose weight or investigations,' Evan snapped as Luke removed the blood-pressure cuff.

'I shan't but you do need to sleep,' Luke said. 'Seriously...'

Evan nodded.

'How long have you had the headache for?'

'Since they told me unless they get a liver in the next seventy-two hours that they were taking him off the list.'

'And when was that?'

'Sixty hours ago.'

Luke didn't make small talk and Evan didn't want it. All he needed now was rest and Luke wrote down his findings and wrote up a prescription. He then went and checked the script with Mary then dispensed it himself and went back to the interview room with a small cup of water.

'Take these now for the headache and the same again when you wake up. And here are some sleeping tablets. Take two tonight,' Luke said. 'Good luck with your son. I'm on in the morning. If you're not feeling better...' Luke amended his words. 'If there's no relief from the headache or if you get chest pain or any other symptoms just come straight back down. Mary will make sure you're seen straight away. I'll be on tomorrow—ask for me.'

'Thank you.'

'Are you walking up to ICU now?' Luke checked. 'I'm on my way there now.'

'I might just go and get some air.'

Usually Luke would just go back to the flat on a night like tonight as he was due in at eight tomorrow.

Luke even thought about doing just that.

But Scarlet was at home.

That gave him even more of a reason to stay at the flat, but it would be unfair to her, Luke knew. And so, before calling for a taxi to take him home, Luke headed up to Intensive Care.

There were a couple of waiting rooms outside the unit that he had to walk past. One was taken up entirely by Anya's team, the other contained the rest of the loved ones of patients on ICU.

It was injustice all the way, Luke thought, but then he hesitated for a moment before using his swipe card to get in as he realised he wasn't here for business reasons only.

He was rarely conflicted—he was here for both personal and professional reasons, though he couldn't really tell David that.

Or could he?

For now, Luke chose not to. He wasn't crossing any lines, he was merely here to catch up on a patient.

He would keep it at that, Luke decided, as he walked over to the vast station where various staff sat writing up notes and checking results as well as taking a quick break. All the patients had a nurse at their bedside and he asked Lorna, the ICU charge nurse, if David was still there.

'He's just in with a patient,' Lorna said. 'He shouldn't be too much longer.'

'How's your night been so far?' Luke asked, and Lorna gave an eye-roll.

'Better than it could have been.' Lorna sighed. 'Thankfully the day staff had the foresight to arrange an extra receptionist to cover tonight. We've got one phone ringing hot solely to enquire about Anya, and it's people using any guise...'

'Such as?'

'Her partner, her lover, a close friend, her aunt...' Lorna turned as someone called her name. 'It would seem that it's her daughter now,' Lorna said, and rolled her eyes once more. 'Again.'

Luke was proud of the staff at the hospital and how they guarded their patients' privacy so fiercely. After a brief pause, Lorna was back. 'You'd think they would get someone with a *real* American accent to call and pretend to be Scarlet.' Lorna gave a wry grin. 'Someone who at least knew their mother's real name.'

'Which is?' Luke asked, because he'd never actually got around to that.

'Anne Portland,' Lorna said. 'Are the press still at the entrance?'

'They are.' Luke nodded. 'Hopefully they'll get bored soon and go.'

'Not a chance,' Lorna said. 'They've just got wind that Scarlet isn't here. I don't know how they found out and I don't want to know either. It didn't come from my staff, that's all I can say.' She had seen it all before and on many occasions. 'Anyway, I've got other things on my mind right now.' She nodded out to the unit. 'Ashleigh—an eighteen-year-old waiting for a liver transplant. We're going to have to take him off the list soon.'

'I just saw his father.'

'Poor man. He's been holding it together for his wife but he's starting to lose it. And on the other hand I've got Anya's people moaning about the coffee and the lack of information.' She looked up as David came over. 'How is he?'

'One word or two?' David asked.

'One,' Lorna said.

'Gutted.'

Luke looked over to the young man they were discussing. He didn't need to be told that Ashleigh was in the third bed along. The young man was a sickly yellow colour and completely emaciated and exhausted, yet he managed to smile at his father as Evan walked back onto the unit.

Evan returned the smile.

God, life could be cruel.

'How are you, Luke?' David asked.

'I'm well,' Luke replied. 'I just thought I'd stop by and see how Anya was doing.' He felt as shallow as hell, especially when David rolled his eyes.

'I never thought you'd be one to jump on the bandwagon.'

'I'm just following up on a patient I thought I was going to lose this morning,' Luke answered.

'Sorry.' David gave a brief shake of his head. 'Long day,' he said, 'and it's going to be an even longer night.'

'You're on call?' Luke checked, and David nodded.

'I'm doing a double.' He got back to Anya. 'There's been no real change with her.' He pulled up Anya's notes on the computer and Luke read through the toxicology results that had come through so far. 'She ticks every box...'

'Yep.' Luke read it with a sinking feeling. It really was starting to look less and less like an accidental overdose, especially coupled with the row that she'd had with Scarlet last night.

'There was some discord with the daughter the night before,' Luke said.

'I saw it in your notes,' David said. 'Scarlet didn't mention it to me, just said she was going to stay with a friend.'

Luke said nothing. The fact there had been an argument was pertinent to Anya's care plan and that was the reason he had noted it.

Where Scarlet was staying wasn't pertinent.

'Thanks for that.' Luke stood, though knew he had to ask David for more than he usually would. 'David, can you call me if there is any change in Anya, either way?'

'Where on the list do you want to be?' David sighed as he headed away from the desk and towards another patient and there was a slightly sarcastic edge to his voice. 'Before or after her manager, the DON, the—'

'Can you call me first?' Luke interrupted.

David stopped walking and looked at Luke and frowned for a moment. It was a very unlikely request from a very unstarstruck Luke.

'I'm asking as a friend,' Luke said.

'Okay.'

'Don't ask any more than that,' Luke said.

'I shan't,' David agreed.

'But you will call me?' Luke checked.

'I shall.'

'And will you pass that on to whoever takes over from you in the morning?'

David nodded. 'I'm here on and off for most of the week. I'll be sure to keep you informed.'

'Thank you.'

Luke said goodnight and then he walked out, past the entourage and then down the corridor and there, walking just ahead of him, was Angie. When he called her name she turned around and, Luke thought, she looked just as tired as he felt.

'How come that you're still here?' Luke checked.

'Full moon,' she said. 'Do you need a lift?'

'I'll be fine. Anyway, I live ages away…'

'Which will give us plenty time to talk, and I prom-ise not to lecture. I can listen, though.' Angie gave a wry smile.

Luke never said very much.

'So what are your plans?' Angie asked as they drove out of the car park.

'No plans really,' Luke admitted. 'I think it's just about giving Scarlet some space.'

'You won't get any space if they find out where she is.'

'We'll see.'

They drove in silence for a while.

'Why *do* you live so far away?' Angie asked when they hit the motorway.

'It's just nice to get away,' Luke answered.

That wasn't the full reason, but Luke kept that to him-self.

'Have you spoken with her private physician?' Angie asked with a sarcastic edge.

'Not yet.' Luke's response was tart as he thought of Vince. 'He's *unavailable* at the moment.'

'I'll bet.'

They were silent for a while but for Luke it was an angry silence, not at Angie, but because all that had gone on in the past was now firing his mind in all directions.

'Did I tell you that Anya once offered me a job as her private doctor?'

'No.'

It still angered him now. 'That was Scarlet's solution, to put me on her mother's payroll and have me be a part of that circus.'

'I think that sounds more like Anya's solution,' Angie said. 'Anyway, she'd soon have fired you when she realised how tight you are with drugs.' Angie smiled. When she'd had her wisdom teeth out Luke had rationed all the decent stuff, but then she stopped smiling at the memory and was serious. 'The baby would have been a part of the circus too.'

'No.' Luke shook his head.

'Of course it would have, and so would you.'

Luke just stared at the road ahead. He'd thought about it, of course he had. Life as Scarlet's partner or ex, access visits played out with the media looking on.

And even if he could have somehow taken it, which he doubted, what about his own family? They had their own lives, their own secrets, their own issues, and he'd have been exposing them too.

No, he couldn't live that life and neither would he have wanted it for his child.

'I'd never have let it come to that,' Luke said.

'Do you really think you could have shielded Scarlet, a pregnant Scarlet at that, from the press?'

'I'd like to have at least had the chance to try.'

'Is this what this is about?' Angie asked as they pulled up at his home.

'No,' Luke said, but then he looked at his house, which felt very different with the knowledge that Scarlet was in there. 'Maybe. Or maybe I'm just trying to give her a break.'

'God knows, she must need one after twenty-five years of it. Her whole life played out in front of the cameras...'

Luke sat there as Angie spoke.

'Poor kid,' she said. 'She's never known anything different.'

'She wanted to, though.'

It was what he had admired so very much about her.

Scarlet had wanted to escape.

She had told him the morning they had made love.

Luke had always laughed at the very notion of love at first sight.

Not now.

But he could not let himself remember that morning if he wanted to get through tonight so he thanked Angie for the lift, got out of the car and said goodnight.

Scarlet was definitely here. Luke could tell from the missing bricks in the low wall of his driveway, which he guessed the car had clipped. The house was in darkness and he wondered if he'd have to knock but, no, the door opened and he stepped in and locked it behind him.

Her scent was there and there were his car keys on the hall table beside the theatre cap and the clogs he had given her to wear, which had been kicked off.

Luke walked through to the kitchen and, no, Scarlet hadn't done his breakfast dishes, he thought with a wry smile as he saw all the evidence of her scrambled eggs. The shells were on the bench; she hadn't even soaked the pan, though he could forgive that one because he always meant to soak his breakfast bowl but never did.

He poured himself a glass of grapefruit juice and sat there for a long moment before heading upstairs.

Luke walked straight past the spare room. He knew that she wouldn't be in there and he was right.

Luke turned on the lights to his bedroom and there Scarlet was, naked in his bed and asleep, but she stirred as he came in and then yelped as he whipped back the duvet.

'Bed,' he said.

'I'm in it.' Scarlet smiled, not remotely fazed that she was stark naked. 'How's Mom?'

'Same,' Luke said, and scooped her up in his arms and carried her down the hall towards the spare room.

'Luke, I want you...'

'No way,' Luke said.

She was trying to rain kisses on his face as her hands went behind his neck, and recall was instant—he was as hard as anything, feeling her all warm and squirming, but there was no way that he'd be sleeping with her.

'Bed.' He dropped her onto the spare one and wished he'd thought to pull back the sheet first because Scarlet lay naked, her arms above her head and every bit as beautiful as he remembered.

More so even.

She had filled out a little bit and there was a jet of pubic hair that hadn't been there last time.

It was now silky and tempting and taunting Luke in his peripheral vision as he tried to meet her gaze.

Still Scarlet refused to meet his eyes.

'How could you sleep with me when you can't even look at me?' Luke asked.

She didn't know how to answer that and she screwed her eyes closed in shame.

'There's no change with your mother.' Luke tried to keep his voice calm and even as he brought her up to date. He tried to be all professional and detached but with an aching hard-on and closer to tears than she could ever know. 'But she's stable.'

'When will we know more?'

'I'll be called if there's any change. Other than that, I'll check on her first thing in the morning. I'll be leaving early tomorrow. Don't answer the phone unless it's me.'

Scarlet nodded. 'Will you come in and see me before you go to work?'

'Why?'

'Because I don't want to have to wait till tomorrow night to see you again.'

There was so much to say, so many questions, but, no,

he couldn't bear to go there just yet so he gave a brief nod instead.

'I'll pop in and say goodbye.' He could not stay a moment longer. 'Good night.'

'How can it be a good night?' Scarlet asked, as she looked at the man who was walking out the bedroom door.

It was the longest, loneliest night for both of them.

It simply felt wrong to be at opposite ends of the hallway but raw was the hurt that kept them apart.

And the hurt was still there the next morning as Luke had his breakfast then made her a coffee and braced himself to go up the stairs.

'Good morning,' Luke said, as she gave him a just-awake smile.

For both of them it was.

Oh, it was awful still, but better than yesterday's had been, and certainly better than the seven hundred and forty-eight that had come before.

She watched as he put her coffee down but then, suddenly embarrassed by her behaviour last night, she covered herself with the sheet as she sat up. 'I don't get why you're cross that I came on to you.'

'I'm not cross,' Luke said. 'Sex isn't going to fix things, Scarlet.'

'I wasn't intending to fix things, just…' She told him the truth. 'I don't want you to change your mind about me staying here and I thought—'

'I didn't bring you here for sex, Scarlet. Did you sleep?'

'I did!' Scarlett sounded surprised. 'Not at first,' she said.

'Nor me.'

'It's a nice room,' Scarlet said, and even if it wasn't the room she would prefer to be in, she looked around the little spare room, pulled open the curtain by the bed and peered into the dark outside and saw a lamppost and beneath it someone walking a dog.

'I'd love to go for a walk.'

'Then go,' Luke said.

'I haven't got any clothes.'

'I'll sort that out today. I know it's probably a bit boring, being cooped up.'

'Oh, I'm far from bored,' Scarlet said. 'I love your home.'

'Thank you,' Luke said. 'So do I.'

He sat down on the bed and she felt relief that he wasn't dashing off.

'How long have you lived here?'

'Nine months,' Luke said. 'It's a bit far out but I like it.'

'I can see why. It was a nice drive, even if I was terrified I was being followed at first.' She pulled a little face. 'I think I scratched your car. I didn't see the wall on your driveway.'

'That's okay.'

'It's quite a scratch actually,' Scarlet said.

'Yeah, and I'm missing a few bricks from my wall,' Luke said. 'I saw.'

'Sorry.'

'It's not a big deal. I did the same when I first moved in.'

And then, when he should have gotten up and left, Luke did what he had to—as she went to reach for her coffee he halted her.

Not her arm. Instead, his hands went to her face.

Scarlet felt the heat of his palms caress her cheeks and then his mouth soft on hers and he kissed her. Oh, how their mouths needed each other's. It was a soft morning kiss and for it, Scarlet knew, she would float better through the day.

She kissed him back, feeling again the lips she'd missed, and so gentle and unexpected was he that Scarlet felt tears sting in her eyes.

It was just a kiss and neither pushed for more.

'Look at me,' Luke said, still holding her face, yet she still would not meet his eyes.

'I can't.'

'You can.'

But she couldn't.

'Have your coffee,' Luke said, and he let her go and handed her mug to her. 'I'll call once I get into work and I know how she's doing.'

Scarlet nodded and he got up off the bed and walked to the door.

'You'll never be able to forgive me, will you?' Scarlet said, and she waited for his terse response, for angry words, for reproach and to be shamed, but instead he turned around.

'Or you me,' Luke said.

He was Dr Responsible.

Boring, some said, not that he cared what others thought—only what she thought of him and his actions.

In something so basic he had let her down.

'That morning...' He watched the colour rise on her cheeks.

It hadn't been the night.

He had kissed her all over and made love to her with his mouth through the night and Scarlet had done the same to him but it wasn't the night they now remembered.

No, it had been just as dawn had arrived that things had changed and moved in ways he had never thought they would...

Luke couldn't think of that now so he turned and walked off.

She heard him go down the stairs and the closing of

the front door, and Scarlet got out of bed and ran onto the landing, still holding her mug. She wanted to call out for him to come back.

But then came the sound of his car starting up and as he drove down the street Scarlet heard the automatic door to the garage close.

She looked down the hall to his bedroom and stood there, and despite the fact the house was cold, she felt warm as she headed into his bedroom.

Luke had left her alone with the memory of them.

CHAPTER EIGHT

'THANK YOU FOR a wonderful night…' Scarlet sat on Luke's stomach and looked down.

That shadow on his jaw was darker now, and his hair was messed up in a way that she liked.

She circled the bruise her mouth had made on his neck and then her fingers moved to the hairs on his chest and she toyed with them. 'It was the best night.'

'It's been great,' Luke agreed.

The lack of condoms hadn't been an issue. They'd found plenty to do without them and now he lay looking up at her as they chatted. 'You don't live in London?' she checked.

'No, I'm just here for an interview.'

'So where do you live?'

'Oxford.'

'With your family?'

'No.' He rolled his eyes at the very thought. 'I was out of there at eighteen.'

'Don't you get on?'

'We do.' He was dismissive and Scarlet frowned.

'Are your parents together?'

Luke nodded.

'How long have they been married?'

'They just had their thirtieth anniversary.'

'Wow!'

He saw her wide eyes as she pictured his perfect life.

'It's not all roses, Scarlet.'

'It sounds it to me.'

And so he let her think that.

Luke let everyone think that.

It wasn't his place to tell.

'So it was your brother's birthday last night?' Scarlet checked.

'Marcus.' Luke nodded. 'He just turned twenty-one.'

'Do you have any other brothers?' Scarlet asked. She wanted to know everything that she could about him.

Luke shook his head. 'I have a younger sister—' Luke started, but Scarlet jumped in.

'I'd love that,' Scarlet admitted. 'I'd give anything to have a sister.'

'It's just you?' Luke checked.

'My mom says we're like sisters.' Now it was she who rolled her eyes.

'Well...' He tried but he couldn't really grasp it. 'I could never see my mum in a nightclub with me.'

'It's embarrassing,' Scarlet admitted, and went a bit pink. 'She gets wasted and the guys chat her up...' She pulled a face that showed her distaste.

Luke thought about his own mother and her love affair with gin. It was bad enough seeing her that way at home— heaven forbid if he had to witness it when out.

'Then she sings,' Scarlet said, and it was the way she said it that had Luke smile.

'Can you sing?'

'Do you really think I'd even try?'

He looked up into shrewd eyes and he wasn't smiling now. This was a young woman who had learnt to never attempt to outshine her mother.

He looked right into her eyes and wondered about all she could be.

'Would you like to sing?' Luke asked.

'No.'

'What would you like to be?'

'To be?' Scarlet frowned. 'Without her, you mean?'

Luke nodded and he watched as the little pink blush that had receded now darkened.

'I've never thought about it,' Scarlet said.

He knew that she was lying and he didn't mind a bit. In fact, he was inordinately pleased that, given her circumstances, Scarlet *had* thought about it, even if she preferred not to reveal her thoughts. And who could blame her? There were secrets in that pretty head, Luke was sure, and no doubt the press would love to know them.

He glimpsed her life again—Scarlet could trust no one, not even the man she was in bed with.

She *could* trust him, Luke thought, even if she didn't know it.

'Do the two of you get on?'

He watched as her eyes narrowed, and he knew she was about to shoot him down, say that of course they did.

'This is just between us,' Luke clarified.

'Of course it is.' Her response was sarcastic and then she met those deep brown eyes and tempered her thoughts. Something about Luke had drawn her to him at the club— his calm disposition at first and then that he'd had no idea who she was had at first been refreshing. Now that he knew, and only wanted her, he made her feel safe.

It would be foolish to let her guard down, Scarlet warned herself. She'd been the victim of pillow talk in the past and yet she could no more imagine Luke selling his story than she could him suddenly sprouting horns.

She might live to regret this, Scarlet thought, but she took a tentative breath and spoke on.

'If I behave we get on.'

'If you don't?'

She shrugged but Luke persisted. 'What happens if you argue?'

'People don't tend to argue with Anya,' Scarlet said.

Luke stayed silent as she prevaricated. It was a survival mechanism, he knew, and it concerned him greatly. He knew she was seriously scarred.

'Ever?'

Scarlet shrugged. 'I choose my battles.' She gave him a smile and moved in for a kiss. 'You're going to be one of them...'

He halted their kiss, wanting to talk some more.

'When you say—'

'You ask too many questions,' Scarlet said. 'We're a one-night stand.'

'Are we?' Luke checked. 'It doesn't have to be.'

'Don't you have a girlfriend?'

Luke frowned. 'I wouldn't be here if I did. I told you we just broke up.'

'When?'

'A month or so ago.'

'That's ages!' Scarlet laughed. 'How long were you to-gether?'

'Two years,' Luke answered. 'What's your longest re-lationship?'

'Oh, I'm too busy to have a relationship,' Scarlet said. 'Anyway, they only want me to get to my mom.'

'Not true,' he said. 'Scarlet...' He wanted to tell her that was utter lies she'd been fed. He wanted many things, not just for Scarlet but for both of them.

Scarlet's thighs gripped him, but her hands were relaxed to him rather than suggestive. His were the same, running over her slender ribs, positioning her a little bit farther back and just enjoying her as they spoke.

'Why did you break up?' Scarlet asked.

'We just did.'

And he was very glad that they had, or he'd have missed this.

He looked up at her smiling mouth. Her face was flushed and pink and her hair was tousled. Luke's eyes moved down over her body. There was a bruise on her left breast from him and her nipples were darker from his attentions.

He didn't answer her question; instead, he put one hand behind her head to pull her down and, with her body angled over his, he went for the other breast.

'I wish we...' Scarlet panted as he licked her breast and then took it deep in his mouth, but she didn't finish saying she wished they had condoms. He was hard against her thigh and she had never wanted someone inside her so badly.

Luke wanted her badly.

But then he remembered he was the sensible one and dragged her turned-on and wanting body to lay by his side. Scarlet felt as if she were floating, with only his arm pinning her down.

They kissed, a kiss that demanded more from both of them, one that had Luke deciding that soon he'd just get dressed and find an all-night store, but now it was Scarlet that halted them.

'Why *did* you break up?'

'Because,' Luke said.

Because he hadn't want to drag her on a bus and make out with her, because he hadn't had to fight not to pull her down onto his aching hardness.

He wanted all of that with Scarlet.

'When you say this doesn't have to be a one-night stand, does that mean you'll call me?' Scarlet asked.

'Of course.'

'When?'

He reached over and handed her his phone and she tapped in her number and then took a photo of herself lying in his arms. 'Send that to me.'

'Okay.'

He did so and Scarlet heard her phone buzz across the room and smiled.

'Do you want to go out tonight?' Luke asked. He was more than happy to miss checkout and spend the day in bed and then take her out but Scarlet shook her head.

'I can't tonight. Anya's performing.'

'So you can't go out because your mother's working?' Luke checked. 'I don't get it.'

'She needs me there when she goes on and all the build-up beforehand,' Scarlet explained. At first she had said it as fact but, resting her head on his chest, the madness of her world was all the clearer for her short six hours away from it.

'Maybe we *could* go out?' Scarlet said. 'Or we could stay in again.'

'Sounds good.'

She thought of telling her mother that she wouldn't be there today, or tonight, and the hell that would break out. And then she thought of the worst scenario—being there for her.

Again.

And again and again.

Panic was starting to hit and she tried to deny it, to just lie there and keep her breathing calm and not ruin what had been a wonderful night.

Feeling the sudden tension in her, Luke pulled her in.

His hand stroked her arm and that, just that, had Scarlet feeling a little better.

It was the nicest sensation she had ever felt, just these soft yet firm strokes and the thud of his heart, and, despite her best attempts to stem them, silent tears started coming out of her eyes.

'Scarlet?' Luke checked, and lifted her chin. And it was then, for Scarlet, that panic truly hit as she revealed a truth she had never dared to.

'I don't want to go back...'

Tears never usually moved him but hers did. He could almost feel her desperation and she turned in his arms and released herself and lay on her back, panting as if she'd just run a race.

'What do you mean?' He came over her and started kissing her tears, and they were talking in whispers as she revealed her secret.

'I don't want to go back to my life. I've been trying to work out for years how I can get away,' she admitted, and then closed her eyes. 'Sorry, too much...'

'No, no,' Luke said, when usually he'd be thinking, *What the hell?*

'I don't know how to, though,' Scarlet admitted. 'Everyone I speak to is employed by her.'

'What about friends?' Luke asked.'

'All of my friends are hers first.'

She lay there rigid beneath him. His legs were on the outside of hers and Luke was up on his elbows, looking down at her, and a more lonely world he could not imagine.

Oh, his family had their own issues, but nothing like this.

And he had friends that went way back.

There were people he could turn to if he chose to.

That he chose not to was his own issue.

'I've run away before but I never get very far,' Scarlet said.

'What do you want?' Luke asked.

'I want,' Scarlet said, 'this.'

He got it that she wasn't talking about them at that point, just normality, and on a cold, wet morning, in a very warm hotel room, it didn't seem an awful lot to ask.

'We'll make it so, then.'

And then she was more honest than Scarlet had ever dared to be. 'I want you.'

'Good,' Luke said, 'because I want you too.'

Those dark brown eyes looked right into hers.

'It will be okay.'

She believed him.

'It will.' His mouth was on her lips and they tasted of hope and his words were so assured. 'I'm here now.'

His kiss deepened and it was like he had opened a tap in her heart and kept filling it.

She had lain there rigid but now she just moved beneath him. Like curling ribbon, her limbs wrapped around him and her lips were in thrall to kisses that were deeper and edgier than last night.

His skin was rough and she craved it. Her tongue matched his and her breasts, which had already had more than due attention, were needy and sore as his thumb tweaked one so expertly that her hips arched as if he had touched her between her legs.

The covers were too hot and heavy but the weight didn't feel like a burden, it just cocooned them. As her hips arched she felt the thick length of him pressed to her groin and stomach and then he moved back so he was between her thighs and she squeezed them tight and he moved into their vice.

She was damp, he was too, and there was an ache for more that rushed between them and her hands went to his buttocks and dug in.

'I want you.' Scarlet had never heard her own voice in that tone. It was determined, it was assured, it was desperate, though.

He moved and she could feel him thick at her entrance and she felt dizzy at the brief feel of him parting her, but as he pulled back she moaned and pressed her fingers tighter into taut muscle and begged him in.

He entered just a little way and those small thrusts had their breathing halting, because if they dared to take in air they might lose the giddy sensation.

Common sense, where was it? Luke wondered, because he had been overtaken by sheer want. She was swollen and aroused and sore for him and when Scarlet sobbed, 'Please,' he drove in hard.

'Oh…' Scarlet was frenzied. She had never been made love to like this, nowhere even close.

He offered the brief lie that he would stop soon and took her over and over, and it felt as if he were exploring her deep inside because knots of nerves awakened and he addressed each one.

He kissed her cheek and there were no more tears as he moved down from his forearms so more of his weight was on her and he scooped his arms under her. Her body was shaking and taut beneath his and he felt the intimate pull of her—she wanted more.

She was coming and claiming him with her thighs wrapping around his waist, and she sobbed out as he drove in harder and she met each thrust.

It wasn't pretty but it felt divine.

The bed was banging, both could hear it, and Luke, who never lost his head, quite simply did.

The feel of her was intense, the sound of them was volatile, like a drive-by shooting was taking place as they exploded one into the other.

Bang.

Bang.

Bang, bang, bang.

Bang, bang, bang, *bang.*

And Luke, who always held back a part of himself, was moaning and shouting and coming deep into her.

The hotel room rattled to their tune, and they were still going.

She came again, just on the tail end of his, and Luke groaned and shot out a final release, and then they collapsed into a void of silence and breaths and hot kisses and promises that made no sense because they'd been together for just a few hours.

Her hair was wild and damp and it felt as if they'd made love in a sauna.

It was hot, sticky sex with no end in sight because he was still inside her.

He moved to pull out but Scarlet gripped him. She gave him no rest, just a slow kiss to recover, and then a deeper kiss as he started to grow within her. But then came a knock on the door.

'Damn.' Luke laughed. 'Breakfast.'

She had no idea in that moment that the knock on the door heralded the end of them.

Scarlet opened her eyes as if someone had just knocked on the door to Luke's bedroom.

Her face was red in his pillow, her sex still twitching as it had that morning, and still she wondered what would have happened if breakfast hadn't come then.

Sometimes she lost herself to her imaginings of how

their worlds might have been had they not been disturbed, but not today. Instead, she remembered how he had climbed from the warm bed, semihard, and had pulled a towel around his hips.

She'd heard the door open and then, after a moment, it had closed and, suddenly remembering what she had done, Scarlet had closed her eyes in regret.

Scarlet could almost hear the rattle of the tray and Luke's tense breathing as he'd slammed it down on a table.

'Scarlet…' His voice was clipped and she could feel his contained fury. 'There are three security guards outside the door…'

It had been the end of them.

The beginning of a very rapid ending and now, two years later, she lay alone in his room.

Last night, Scarlet had thought she had no more tears left to cry over them.

But of course she did.

CHAPTER NINE

THERE WERE DIVERSION signs in place as Luke drove into the hospital.

'What's going on?' Luke asked, winding down his window and speaking with Geoff.

'One of the news vans broke down at the entrance to the staff car park,' Geoff said. 'At least, that's what they've said has happened. I think they're trying for a view of ICU.'

'Call the police,' Luke said. 'Get them moved.'

Instead of parking in his usual spot underground, Luke took for ever to find a space.

The press were still outside the foyer and security and other staff who were arriving for their shifts were looking very unimpressed with it all.

As was Luke.

Instead of heading straight into A and E, Luke headed up to ICU to catch David before he started handover.

Anya's people were still there but their numbers had thinned down.

In the other waiting room he saw Ashleigh's parents. Evan was sitting with his head in his hands as the mother paced.

When Luke stepped into the unit he found out why.

The space where Ashleigh's bed had been was empty

and Luke walked over to Lorna, who was just coming off the phone.

'Did he get a liver?'

'He did.' Lorna nodded. 'He just went to Theatre.'

He saw that Lorna, who was possibly the toughest of the tough, was on the edge of tears.

'Ashleigh's been in and out of here for the last six months. It's wonderful to see him get this chance.' Lorna shook her head. 'I'm not going to be able to sleep.'

'Well, you need to,' Luke said, 'so you can be back here tonight to look after him.'

'Please, God,' Lorna said.

He glanced over at Anya. 'How has she been?' Luke asked.

'She's had a stable night, apart from a spike in her temperature, but we were anticipating that. David's going to be a while. He took Ashleigh down to Theatre, just to see him put under. He's not staying for the op, though. He should be back soon.'

'That's fine,' Luke said.

He'd call back in on his way home, Luke decided, but for now he made his way down to his own department and worked through his list. But at ten, just before he started the fracture clinic, he called Scarlet.

Luke wasn't sure if she'd be up but he didn't know when he would get a chance to call again so he rang three times and hung up then called again.

Scarlet had spent a long time crying and her eyes were still watery as she lay in his bed and stared at the ringing phone at the bedside.

It rang off on the third ring and then rang again and she picked up the phone.

'Is that you?'

'It is,' Luke said. 'How are you?'

'How's Mom?' Scarlet asked, by way of answer.

'She's stable. There's no real change.'

'Is that good or bad?'

'It's good for now,' Luke said. 'Have you been crying?'

'A bit,' she admitted.

'Well, your mum's doing as well as can be expected and...'

Scarlet listened to his soothing words. She could let Luke think she was crying about her mother.

Later on she might be.

Just not now and she told him so.

'Luke, I wasn't crying about my mom. Seeing you, being in your home, well, it's kind of brought it all back. Not that it ever went away. I'm sorry for what I did—'

'Scarlet,' Luke interrupted. 'Let's not do this over the phone.'

'When, then?'

He didn't answer.

She lay in his bed when she should be sitting by her mother's.

'Do you think I should come in and see her?'

'That's up to you.'

'I know it is, I'm just asking for your take.'

'Okay, then, I think you need some time.' Luke was honest with his answer. He had seen Anya's lab results and it was looking less and less like the accidental overdose the spin doctors were trying to say it had been.

'What if she wakes up and I'm not there?' Scarlet asked.

'Yeah, well, I know how bad that feels,' Luke said, and it was the first real glimpse of his temper weighted against them because he abruptly rang off.

Luke stared at the phone.

He told himself to pick it up and pretend that he'd been cut off.

But as he sat there staring, he was reliving it too.

Not the nice part before, just the hell of afterwards, when he had walked back into the hotel room.

'What are they doing out there?' he'd demanded.

There had been three guys standing right outside the door and he'd recognised a couple of them from the club!

Scarlet hadn't fully understood his anger. 'I texted them to let them know where I was.'

'You. Did. What?'

Each word was an accusation in itself and Scarlet rose in the bed to her own defence. 'I didn't want people worrying.'

'So while we were...' His anger was mounting at the thought that her bodyguards had been standing outside and would have heard the noise they'd made. Worse, that Scarlet thought this completely normal incensed him. 'You told me that you wanted a night away from it all.'

'And I did, but I didn't want to make trouble.'

'You said—'

'You have no idea what my life is like,' Scarlet shouted.

'I'm trying to understand.'

'Well, you can't!' Scarlet could not take it in that he was angry at her. It spun her into a panic and she started crying. There was a knock on the door and then another, and, despite Luke telling her to leave it, Scarlet opened the door to say that she was okay. But, given she was crying, her bodyguards came in.

'What the hell...?' Luke exploded at the intrusion. He was furious at the insult their coming in inferred—as if he might have been about to hurt her.

'So you'll stand outside while she's having sex and then interrupt a discussion?' Luke shouted at the burliest one, and what had him raging was that Scarlet was standing there naked.

'Get back in the bed,' Luke shouted. He wanted her covered, he wanted this audience gone, but she misread his anger and dressed instead and within moments she was gone.

And now, two years later, he sat staring at the phone.

Scarlet couldn't deal with anger or arguments, and no wonder. He could see that now, he just hadn't been able to then.

Today was the second time in their history that he had hung up on her.

He didn't want to discuss the other time but knew that soon they'd have to.

Luke didn't take the easy way out now.

He picked up the phone and called her back.

CHAPTER TEN

THE PHONE RANG again and she didn't wait for three rings but picked it up straight away.

Had he missed her for all of these two years?

Was that what he'd just said?

The brusque tone of his voice gave her no clue.

And if he was angry, why was he calling her back?

'Sorry about that,' Luke said.

'Did you just hang up on me?' Scarlet asked.

'Yep,' he admitted, rather than saying they had been cut off, which was what he would normally have done. Luke had never known anyone like Scarlet, or the feelings she evoked in him. He couldn't remember hanging up the phone on anyone before. He was so obstinate at times that it was usually the other way around. 'I'm back now.'

Scarlet smiled. 'I'm glad.'

'We'll talk properly later,' Luke said. 'I know we have to but not over the phone...'

'I get it,' Scarlet said.

He got back to the subject of her mother. The reason for his call.

'She's not going to be waking up today. They're keeping her under for a day or two more at least and when she does wake up she'll be drowsy,' Luke rather more patiently explained. 'We'll cross that bridge when we come to it.'

'Okay,' Scarlet said, and then she said the nicest thing, Luke thought, when there must be so much on her mind. 'How are you?'

Fine, he was about to say. 'A bit tired,' Luke admitted. 'I'm going to finish up early today.'

'That's good.'

'What are you doing now?' Luke asked.

'I'm still in bed,' Scarlet said. She just omitted to mention whose bed she was in! 'What about you?'

'I'm just about to start a clinic so I have to go. Do you need anything from the shops?'

Indeedy she did!

Luke finished at three and by four-thirty he was in the supermarket to purchase his fugitive's supplies.

Quinoa?

He'd never even walked down the health-food aisle.

Kale?

His mother used to put that in soup! No way.

And she could have button mushrooms, like the rest of the world, Luke decided.

He threw in some eggs but he did make a small concession and got the organic, free-range ones—he'd been meaning to switch to them for a while anyway.

Luke stopped by the meat section but then looked back at the list. Did Scarlet even eat meat?

Yes! Luke remembered the breakfast they had ordered and never eaten but memories like that were too risky to have right now so he moved through to the clothes section.

There wasn't much choice.

He tried to guess her size and guessed she'd be the smallest so he bought some leggings, a couple of baggy tops and a pair of jeans.

And, thinking of the boots she had been wearing, which

weren't really made for walking, he bought some slip-on shoes.

Then he headed over to the underwear section.

Maybe not, Luke thought as he stared at a pack of five-for-the-price-of-three knickers.

He paid and left the supermarket but instead of going to his car he walked down the main street of the village and into a small boutique, which was a first for Luke.

'It's my partner's birthday…'

Trefor's wife smiled.

Trefor was the local policeman and Luke could never remember his wife's name. It was one of those names he should know by now but it was a bit late in the day to ask.

'Oh, well, we'll have to get her something nice, then.'

'Not too nice,' Luke said.

'How have you been, Luke?'

'Very well,' Luke answered, embarrassed that she knew his name.

'What size is your partner?'

'I'm not sure,' Luke said. 'She's very slim.'

'Well, do you know her bust size?'

'Small,' Luke answered, glad that he at least he knew that!

'Do you know, Trefor was just saying the other day that I should put the store online. Apparently men don't like coming in.'

'No,' Luke agreed.

'These are nice,' Trefor's wife said, 'though not *too* nice, and they've got a bit of stretch in them.'

It was very possibly amongst the most uncomfortable twenty minutes of Luke's life but, having made his purchases and thanking her, Luke was just about to head for home when Trefor came through the door.

'Hi, Luke.'

'Hi, Trefor.' Luke was about to head out but then he thought better of it. 'Trefor, I've got a friend staying with me.' He told him who it was. 'I'm hoping—'

'No problem,' Trefor said. 'I'll keep an eye out. Thanks for letting me know.'

Finally he was home.

The house felt nicer with Scarlet there. It wasn't just the warmth from the heater that changed things when Luke came in, it was Scarlet coming out of the lounge, wearing one of his shirts and also a smile.

'I missed you,' Scarlet said.

'Well, I'm here now.'

'How is she?'

'Much the same,' Luke said, and he looked at her worried expression. 'Do you want me to take you in to see her?'

'I don't know,' Scarlet admitted. She could see that Luke was exhausted but that wasn't the real reason she was holding back.

Here she could think.

Beside her mother's bedside she couldn't.

'No rush,' Luke said, sensing her quandary. 'She's stable.'

'I should be there, though.'

He didn't know what to say because his truth was that he didn't want her near that woman, but he held back from saying so.

'I'm going to go and get changed,' Luke said.

He went upstairs and put the underwear he had bought her in his wardrobe, pulled on some jeans and a jumper and then came back downstairs, carrying a mug, and not in the best of moods.

Scarlet had gone and the shopping still stood in the hallway.

'Scarlet!' he called, and she came out of the lounge.

'What?'

'I don't have servants and I've been at work all day.' He gestured to the bags and then held up a mug. 'What's a half-empty mug of coffee doing by my bed?'

'Maybe you were in a rush and didn't finish it?'

'I don't drink coffee.'

'Oh.'

'Were you in my bed this morning?'

It annoyed him that she smiled and nodded. 'It's more comfortable.'

It concerned him that he was fighting not to smile back.

That's what Scarlet did to him, though.

'Don't do that again!' he warned as she picked up the bag that held the lettuce and other heavy goods and carried it through to the kitchen.

'What did you do today?' Luke asked.

'Not much. I read some of your textbooks,' she admitted.

He was putting away the shopping and he held up a bottle of wine and she nodded.

'Do you like your job?' Scarlet asked.

'I love it,' Luke told her. 'I can't imagine my life without it.' He looked over at her. 'Would you like to be a midwife?'

'I just said it that night for something to say.'

'You said it again when you spoke to Angie.'

'Angie?'

'She's a friend.'

'The woman in the elevator!' Scarlet laughed as she remembered the conversation. 'I thought she was about to call Security on me for being an impostor.'

'No, that's Angie just trying to work things out.' He turned and gave her a smile. 'Lucy Edwards.'

Her cheeks went pink and then she told him something. 'I've seen babies being born.'

'When?'

'In Africa,' Scarlet said. 'The first time I went they gave me a private tour of the maternity ward. I didn't want to leave.'

'Really?'

Scarlet nodded.

'I went back again last year.'

'I saw,' Luke said, but without malice. 'Did you visit the maternity ward again?'

'I did, and I saw some babies being born. They'd told me they needed a drug called oxytocin for the women and we brought loads with us.'

'That's good.'

It was good and he turned and smiled.

'Here…' He tossed her a bag of clothes and he started to make dinner as Scarlet went through them.

'I'm not wearing these…'

'I thought the intention was for you to blend in.'

'Supermarket jeans?' Scarlet pulled a disgusted face and then she took out the shoes. 'These are men's shoes.'

'They're not.'

'If I wear these, people will think I'm a lesbian.'

Luke rolled his eyes and carried on chopping as Scarlet brought the subject back to the one they'd been discussing.

'Anyway, I don't think I'd be a very good midwife.'

'Why not?'

'I just don't.'

'Well, there are plenty of other things…' He glanced at her. He could see she was pensive and he could feel the shift in the light-hearted mood and knew she was thinking about their baby.

He loathed it that he carried on with preparing dinner but he did.

That was him.

'I thought you hadn't called me,' Scarlet said, touching on the subject that had to be faced but not yet, Luke thought, not with so much other stuff going on.

'It was only when I tried to ring you. After...' Scarlet sat and looked at his tense back. 'That I realised they'd blocked your number. Till then I thought you hadn't tried to call.'

'Well, I did,' Luke said. 'Over and over and then, when I couldn't get through, I arranged for some time off.'

'I didn't know.'

Luke said nothing. He didn't know what to say so he threw the mushrooms in the wok. Then he glanced up at the kitchen window. It was already dark and he could see her strained features in her reflection.

He was so loath to discuss it, though he knew he had to at least try, and he took the less easy option for the second time that day.

'Why didn't *you* call *me*?' Luke asked, and turned around. 'Why didn't you at least try and call to discuss things with me?'

'Because I was being selfish to land this on you, apparently. Because you had your life planned out and it sure as hell didn't include me.'

'Is that what she said?'

Scarlet didn't immediately answer. 'I was reminded that in two months' time I was going to Africa again. It's my favourite place and I was reminded that I could do a lot more good there...'

'Your mother said that?'

'Everyone said it.'

And by everyone she meant everyone, Luke thought. Every person Scarlet came into contact with was on her mother's payroll. He thought of his own confusion at the time. Everything that had seemed so simple in the bedroom, when it had just been the two of them, had been muddied beyond recognition.

He'd spoken to Angie about the pregnancy and had listened to her objective thoughts, then there had been a long conversation with a friend from rugby he'd gone to school with who had been through similar. He had given somewhat less than objective advice and had suggested that Scarlet was after a meal ticket.

Luke had omitted to mention Scarlet's name and her millions but those words had rattled.

It had been a one-night stand. He'd been aware at the start that they wouldn't last and he'd wondered if he had merely been an escape route.

Luke had looked at his parents' crap marriage, a couple who were together for the children and appearances' sake.

He'd had so many people and life experiences to draw on.

Scarlet had had Anya and her empire.

'Anyway,' Scarlet suddenly said, 'I couldn't do that to my child.'

'What?'

'Give it my life.'

'I wouldn't have let that happen!' Luke responded. 'All you had to do was pick up a phone or get on a plane...' He was trying to keep his voice from rising. Hell, there was a reason he hadn't wanted to discuss this now. It was too raw, and he was exhausted, not just from work but from the impact of having Scarlet back in his life.

He watched her stand.

'Don't walk off!' Luke warned.

'Oh, you can talk!'

'Meaning?'

'It's a shame we're not on the phone. You could just hang up!'

'Scarlet…' He didn't get to finish—the wok was spewing black smoke and he dragged it off the hob, but Scarlet wasn't sticking around to eat, or discuss, charred ruins.

'I don't want dinner,' Scarlet said. 'I'm going to bed.'

Yet there was no relief when she walked out of the room and up the stairs. Words needed to be said.

Dinner was stuffed so he poured a glass of wine and sat there, just staring out at the darkness, until the phone rang.

He took a call from his mother, reminding him about tomorrow and that they'd be there around four but couldn't stay for long.

Good.

He was in no mood for happy families and pretending that thirty-two years of marriage was anything to celebrate when he knew what a sham it was.

Not when he could hear Scarlet crying upstairs.

They were different tears. In fact, he couldn't hear them, just the pad of her feet and the turn of a loo roll and Scarlet blowing her nose once she was back in the spare room.

Luke had learnt to stay back, he'd been told to stay back, to hold in the important stuff and let people live their own lives.

This time he chose not to listen to that ingrained advice and a little while later he made a very long walk and knocked at her door.

'What?' Scarlet lay in bed, surrounded by balls of scrunched-up loo roll.

'I brought you some dinner.'

'I don't want it.'

'Come on,' he said, and then waited till she sat up and put the tray down on her lap. She stared at mushrooms on toast and a glass of wine.

'Aren't you cross?'

'I'm not cross,' Luke said. 'Even if I was, I'm not going to...' He was about to make a joke about withholding food but stopped himself. He could remember her saying that no one won with Anya and he guessed Scarlet flouncing off to her room would have been the only protest she could make.

And he was quite sure they'd leave her there hungry.

'Do you want to talk?' he offered.

'So you can hate me some more?'

'I don't hate you,' Luke said.

'It's okay if you do.' Scarlet gave a tight shrug. 'I hate you too sometimes.'

'Because?'

'Because you've got it all together, because the only mistake you ever made was me.'

'I've made plenty of mistakes, Scarlet, and you weren't one of them.' He came and sat on the bed. 'But, yes, I should have been more careful.'

'Yes, you should have been and so should I,' Scarlet shouted. 'But you're careful now, aren't you?'

'Meaning?'

'How many women since me?'

And he could fudge numbers or say, *Oh, they meant nothing*, or just ride it out, but he answered with the truth. 'Too many,' he admitted, and then he made himself ask the same when usually he would tell himself it was none of his business and back off. 'How about you?'

'Are you serious?'

Very.

He'd seen the smiling photos, the tour of Africa, the red carpet with gleaming plastic men by her side, and he'd tried, God knew, he'd tried to get past the hype, but sometimes, yes, it had felt as if she'd simply carried on without a backward glance.

'You really think I just pulled my knickers back up and carried on...'

'Sometimes,' he admitted, and held his breath, not sure they were strong enough for voicing the truth.

'Well, you're wrong,' Scarlet said. 'You're the one who carried on.' She rose up in the bed and the tray came with her, but she just tossed it to the floor, furious. 'I called you, Luke, and when I told you what I'd done, what did you do, what did you say? Nothing!'

'I didn't want to say the wrong thing.'

'And so you said precisely nothing!' She rose up farther and she pushed on the chest that was so strong but so immovable. 'Believe me, Luke, there was nothing you could have said that I wasn't thinking about myself. I was twenty-three, a woman, I should have been able to know my own mind...'

There were times Luke regretted his inability to speak up, to voice the thoughts in his head or the feelings that ate at him, and one minute ago had been one of those times. Instead, he was glad now that he had held on because the floodgates opened and she beat at him, and raged at him, except it wasn't about him, and Luke knew that.

He had known when he'd walked in the door that her loathing was aimed at herself.

'I listened to them and I shouldn't have.' She raged and raged. 'I'd rather you'd called me a bitch than stay quiet.'

'Really?' Luke took her arms and then he took her chin and still she would not meet his eyes. 'If that's the sort of reaction you were hoping for, Scarlet, then you really are with the wrong guy.' Now she looked at him and she saw those lovely brown eyes she had trusted so much and still did, and she saw tears in them too. 'I didn't know what to think, let alone say,' Luke admitted. 'I was on the way to the airport when you called...'

She started to cry but it was on him this time.

And Luke said nothing, not because he didn't know what to say now but because all she wanted was to cry and be comforted without agenda. And when she'd finished, when there were many more little balls of loo roll added to her pile, it was Scarlet who admitted that she didn't want to talk.

'Fair enough,' Luke said. 'We'll try again when you're ready.'

She looked from his chest to the floor and saw the lovely second dinner he had made dressing the carpet.

'I'll get it,' Luke said.

Scarlet lay back on the pillow when he left quietly and then looked over at the massive wine stain on the carpet and thought about how she'd thrown the tray and shouted. She tried to work out how on earth she could face him tomorrow when there was a knock at the door.

'Third time lucky,' Luke said, and he came in with a tray.

It was completely unexpected and the nicest thing anyone had ever done for her because she really was starving.

No wine this time. Instead, there was a lovely mug of milk and cinnamon and lots of slices of buttery toast smothered in jam.

'Where are the mushrooms?' Scarlet asked.

She'd never ended a row on a smile.

CHAPTER ELEVEN

SOMETHING WAS WRONG.

Scarlet woke and opened the curtain and she looked out at the streetlight and then lay back on the pillow.

The house was cold, even with the heating on. She hadn't felt warm since she'd arrived in England.

She thought of her mother and their row, and whatever had gone on between them, Scarlet wanted to see her.

It wouldn't be fair to ask Luke. He'd had a couple of glasses of wine and was exhausted, she knew that.

She recalled his words—visiting her mother didn't have to be a big deal.

What if she did what he said, went in through the maternity entrance?

The clothes he had bought her really were awful but she put them on and wrote a note and left it on the hall table.

'Gone to see Mom.'

It was an easy drive. There were some roadworks but in less than an hour the hospital came into view. She bypassed the main entrance, indicated for Maternity and parked the car. As she got out Scarlet saw a couple walking towards the door, where they buzzed at the entrance. She walked over quickly.

'Here,' Scarlet said, and held the door open for them as the woman doubled over.

'Thanks.'

She was in.

Her heart was pounding but Scarlet told herself she was doing nothing wrong but then she saw a security guard walking towards her.

'Can I help you?'

'I'm here to see my mother.'

'You can't wander around the hospital at night.'

'The emergency consultant told me if I used the maternity entrance…'

'Scarlet?'

She nodded.

'Geoff.' He gave her a smile. 'Remember?'

Now she did.

'Just wait there,' Geoff said.

He made a phone call and then came back. 'This way.' They chatted as they walked. 'You've saved me a right old drama,' Geoff told her. 'The press have been awful. I've told the ICU staff and they said to bring you up in the theatre lift, which will take you straight onto the unit.'

He went with her but when Scarlet arrived on ICU it was like stepping into a spaceship, but then a woman came over and gave her a smile.

'I'm Lorna.'

'I just wanted some time with her.'

'Of course you do,' Lorna said. 'Did you want to speak with a doctor first?'

'No.' Scarlet shook her head. 'I just want to see her. Is anyone with her?'

'They're all outside,' Lorna said.

It was all very low-key. There were a few other relatives sitting with their loved ones. The curtains weren't drawn as it was break time and the staff were thinner on the ground, Lorna explained.

'I can close them if you need me to. I'll call Ellie back from her break.'

There was no need.

Scarlet sat there and held her mother's hand and was brought a plastic cup of hot chocolate and a packet with two biscuits in.

'Your mum?' a man sitting nearby asked, and Scarlet nodded.

'Who are you here with?'

'My son. He's been in Theatre all day. I've just got in to see him now. I'm Evan.'

'Scarlet.' She smiled.

'I know!' Evan rolled his eyes. 'They're all out there, trying to work out where you are. Good for you!' he said. 'Ashleigh, my son, likes you. He was very fed up that he never got to see you!'

Scarlet laughed.

They chatted.

Not a lot but about how nice the hot chocolate was, how good the staff were.

How scary it was to be here.

'My wife's just gone for a sleep. I had to get some sleeping tablets,' Evan admitted. 'Never taken anything in my life but they did the trick. I thought I was dreaming when I woke up and heard he had a liver.'

'How long has Ashleigh been sick?' Scarlet asked.

'Since he was born,' Evan told her. 'We had a few good years when he turned eleven, but the last year has been the toughest. What about your mum?'

And she was about to make her usual small talk, or smile and say just how wonderful everything was.

Here wasn't the place to, though.

Lies made no difference in the ICU, Scarlet guessed.

It wasn't just the patients who were exposed to serious diagnoses.

'She's been sick for a very long time too,' Scarlet admitted.

'It takes its toll, doesn't it?' Evan said, and she nodded.

'Hot chocolate helps,' Scarlet said. She just sipped on her warm drink and held her mum's hand and then, when the clock nudged three, guessing Luke might need the car early, she stood and gave her mum a kiss on the cheek.

'I love you.'

Scarlet did.

I love you not.

Sometimes.

She just had to love herself more.

'I hope he's improved in the morning,' Scarlet said to Evan.

'Thanks, love.'

And then she offered something stupid, something silly and fun for when Ashleigh woke up, but it made Evan smile.

God knew, he needed it.

The charge nurse called for Geoff to walk her back down and she nodded in the direction of Luke's car.

'I'm fine now,' Scarlet said. 'Thank you.'

'Next time, page the head of security. It's usually me at night,' Geoff said.

'Thanks.'

Scarlet drove home, or rather to Luke's home, feeling better.

Not brilliant but better.

A part of her wanted to turn off the motorway. To simply drive to the cottage that was supposed to have been her haven while she sorted out her head with the luxury of time that had been denied to her now.

How did she tell her mother now that she was still leaving her?

How could she face the impossible conversations that were to come with Luke? And then there were his parents coming later today. Maybe he'd welcome her disappearing?

Scarlet wanted to curl up into a ball and for the world to sort itself out before she came back.

It wasn't going to, though.

The garage door opened as she approached and, hell, England was cold, Scarlet thought. Even the garage was freezing.

The house felt only marginally warmer.

Her note was still there on the table and her midnight adventure had paid off.

She went up to her room and stripped off her clothes then looked at the bed and simply couldn't face getting in. She wanted Luke, not for anything other than who he was and because of where she'd just been.

Scarlet padded down the hall and pushed open the door and there was Luke, deeply asleep. He hadn't even noticed she'd gone, Scarlet knew.

She slipped into the bed and moved straight over to him.

'You're frozen,' Luke said, and pulled her in closer.

Just that.

He stroked her arm as he had once before, and it was as if it was normal that she lie in his arms.

It was.

Luke pulled the covers over her shoulders and went straight back to sleep.

A sleep so deep that Luke even struggled to wake to his alarm. Instead, it blurred into the sound of ambulances or IVs alarming, and then he prised his eyes open and felt Scarlet wrapped around him.

Where it felt she belonged.

CHAPTER TWELVE

HE TURNED OFF the alarm but didn't have the energy to tell her to get back to her own bed, and neither did he want her to get out.

He knew she was awake, he could feel her lashes blinking on his chest.

'Are you okay?' Luke asked.

'No,' Scarlet admitted, and then she said what she'd wanted to when they'd been in the kitchen, as if hours hadn't passed since then. 'I didn't know what to do, Luke.'

Hours might have passed but he knew what was on her mind. 'Tell me.'

'You have to go to work.'

'No.' He did but some things were more important.

'And we can't storm off to bed,' Luke pointed out, 'given we're in it, so maybe we can try and talk.' There were so many details missing, ones he had thought he'd prefer not to know. But that had been when he had thought her callous. 'What was your mother like when you told her?'

'Fine,' Scarlet said from the depths of his chest. 'At first. I had toothache once and she handled it in pretty much the same way—you'll be fine, Vince can take care of that for you. That's when I rang you. I knew we'd ended badly and that I shouldn't have told Troy where I was but—'

'Forget about that now.'

'When you said to come here, that we'd talk and work things out…' She felt stupid explaining it. 'I don't keep my own passport, Sonia does. I didn't know how to get on a plane unless it was my mother's jet. I wanted to, though. I told my mother that I wanted to keep the baby and that I was going to England to speak with you. She went crazy. I didn't get it. I pointed out that she was a single parent and at least I knew who the father was.'

'What did she say to that?'

'She slapped me and told me how ungrateful I was, that, yet again, she had to sort me out. They had a crisis meeting about me. That's when I called you again. She wanted you to come and work for her, alongside Vince.'

'Scarlet, I could never do that.' Luke was honest. 'I wanted to be with you and I wanted us to work out how. I could have accepted some attention and a change to my life but I could never work for your mother.'

'I understand that but when you just dismissed it out of hand…'

'Scarlet, medicine is important to me. I take it very seriously and I could never be paid to prescribe, ever.'

'It seemed like the only way.'

'We'd have worked on finding other ways.'

'And then you didn't call back.'

'I did,' Luke said. 'I was going crazy. I spoke to Angie, and to a friend whose girlfriend, well, his wife now, had got pregnant. I asked my boss if I could take a couple of weeks off. He didn't want to give it to me, given that I'd only been working there for a few days. I told him he could have my notice if he wouldn't give me time off. I was on my way to the airport when you called.'

He'd never forget it.

First there had been relief at hearing her voice when she'd finally called. *I'm on my way,*' he had said.

'*There's no need, it's been taken care of.*'

He'd driven straight into the back of someone.

'I heard the other driver shouting,' Scarlet admitted. 'Then I listened while you moved the car and swapped details and then you came back to the phone.

'*Are you still there?*' he had asked.

'*Still here,*' Scarlet had replied, and then had come the agony of him ringing off.

'I'd just got back from the clinic.'

'Did anyone go with you?'

'Mom,' Scarlet said.

So no one helpful, then, Luke thought.

'She was all nice to me afterwards. I was a mess and she had Vince see me and he put me on antidepressants. I didn't take them. I think I was right to be sad.' Scarlet thought back to that very difficult year. 'I knew things had to change and I also knew they were watching me. I picked up a bit when I found out she was going on tour again and that we'd be coming here.'

'Were you going to call?'

She didn't answer straight away. How could she have landed on him not just herself but all her hopes and dreams? How could she have told him about the shiny, poised, together person she had hoped to be when next she saw him?

'I don't know,' Scarlet said instead.

It hurt to hear that. He'd spent the last few months wondering if she would get in touch and to now to hear that she hadn't made up her mind cut deep.

'What would you have done?' Scarlet asked. 'If I'd called?'

'I guess it would have depended how the conversation went,' Luke admitted. 'But...' He couldn't.

She *hadn't* called.

'Tell me.'

'No.' Luke shook his head.

They were nowhere near ready for that. They might never be.

'I hate it that you went through it on your own. I mean, I know you had your mum...' He tried to be polite but Scarlet gave a low mirthless laugh at his effort.

'She didn't come in. Actually, there was a really nice nurse. I thought they'd be horrible,' she admitted. 'I was a bit of a wreck but she really was lovely to me.'

'I would hope so.'

'She was.' Scarlet still sounded surprised. 'I got very upset afterwards. I knew I'd made a mistake and she spoke to me for ages. She said that one day I'd be able to move on and that I didn't have nothing, that I'd learn from it...'

And it killed him to hear her say she'd thought she had nothing and he was very glad of that nurse who had taken the time with her on such a difficult day.

'And I have,' Scarlet said. 'Which is why I blew up the other day at my mother.'

'Can you tell me about the row?' Luke asked, and Scarlet nodded.

'I told her that I was leaving and she laughed and said I wouldn't last five minutes without her.'

His hand was still stroking her hair.

'I said that I had you,' Scarlet admitted, and she started to cry. 'I didn't know if I did, I guessed not, but I was just trying to get away...'

'I know that.'

'And she said you wouldn't want me, given all I'd done, and then I got angry,' Scarlet said. 'Really angry.'

Now his hand was on her arm, the way it had been that morning, stroking her arm gently and firmly, and there was nothing that she couldn't tell him.

'I said that she'd always been jealous of me and that the reason she didn't want me to keep my baby was because she didn't want the spotlight on me and the "Grandma Anya" headline.' Scarlet looked up at him. 'I'm just sorry it took me so long to work that out.'

'I'm amazed that you could work it out,' Luke said. 'Sometimes I think my family is complicated but…'

He stopped.

She was used to it.

Luke always held back.

'It's just as well that we'll never make it.' Scarlet smiled. 'You could hardly have me meet them.'

'They're coming this afternoon.' Luke sighed. 'It's their wedding anniversary so they're stopping by on their way down to London for a long weekend.'

'Do you want me hide in the bedroom?'

'I don't want to hide you, Scarlet,' Luke said. 'Don't you get that?'

She didn't.

CHAPTER THIRTEEN

LUKE WALKED INTO ICU and nodded to Evan and then he looked over to where Anya lay.

On the morning she had come into Emergency it had taken almost everything that Luke had in him to treat her as just another patient.

He wondered if he could do that if she came in now. He hoped so but right now he was so angry that he truly didn't know.

'We're going to try and rouse her later this afternoon.'

It was a different anaesthetist on this morning.

'Did David pass on my message?'

'He did,' Craig said. 'I'll call you with any changes.'

'Thanks.'

'Lorna spoke with daughter last night,' Craig added. 'She's aware of what's going on and—'

'She spoke with the daughter?' Luke was horrified at any leak in information and tried to sort it out. 'How did Lorna know it was her?'

'Because she came in.' Craig gave him a wide-eyed look. 'Lorna wouldn't speak to just anyone.'

'I know that.'

A nurse came past and started laughing. 'Go and ask Evan if you don't believe him.'

'Evan?'

'Over there.'

Luke looked over and there was Evan, doing his cross-word. Luke made his way over to him. 'How are you doing?'

'A lot better than I was the last time I spoke to you,' Evan admitted, and he saw Luke go to open his mouth. 'I'll make an appointment with my GP about my blood pressure.'

'Good man,' Luke said. 'I hear that you had a visitor last night.'

'Don't tell that lot.' Evan winked and nodded towards the exit door behind which Anya's entourage sat. He took out his phone. 'Lovely lady…' He glanced at his son, who was asleep. 'Ashleigh laughed when I showed him this morning.'

Luke looked at Evan's phone and for all he hated this type of thing, now it made him smile.

There was Scarlet, looking very unlike Scarlet. Not a scrap of make-up and her hair was wild and she was wearing a very baggy jumper and one of his shirts and smiling with Evan into the camera.

'How long was she here?' Luke asked.

'A couple of hours.' And then he looked over at Anya and he said exactly the same as Angie had. 'Poor kid.'

Luke worked for a couple of hours and then he called home in the familiar style and she answered the phone.

'Sorry,' Scarlet said, peeling her eyes open. 'I was asleep.'

He thought of her driving through the night and then coming back to his bed but he didn't let on that he knew.

'Are you up to going out for a walk?'

'Of course.'

'My parents are dropping by about four. I'll be home before then but I need something…'

'What?'

'Biscuits.'

Scarlet frowned.

'Biscuits?' she checked, because where she was from you ate them for breakfast and with gravy. 'You're going to give them biscuits?'

And then Luke remembered there were so many differences between them.

'Cookies.'

'Why?'

'Because they'll want a cup of tea. We're polite like that,' Luke said with an edge.

'You want me to buy cookies for their anniversary?'

'If you've got time.'

'Ha-ha.'

'Do you have any money?' Luke asked.

'I do.'

'Because there's some in the drawer by my...' Luke hesitated. There were some other things he didn't want her to see in the drawer by his bed. It was too late for that, though.

'I've already found them,' Scarlet said. 'I snooped the first day I was here.'

'Well, beside them is some cash.'

'I'll treat you,' Scarlet said and, suddenly too angry for words, she rang off.

Luke called back.

'Did you just hang up on me?'

'I did.'

'Good for you.'

He liked it that she could argue, that she was starting to find her voice.

'I've got a present for you,' Luke said.

'Really?' Scarlet frowned. 'What?'

'Go and open my wardrobe.'

Scarlet got up and Luke sat there hearing her swear at how cold it was, even thought he'd left the heater on high, and trying not to imagine her streaking naked across his bedroom.

'Where?' she asked.

'There's a bag at the bottom.'

Scarlet peeled it open with delight and pulled out all the lovely knickers and bras. 'Are these for me?'

'Scarlet, if I'm hiding a bag of ladies' underwear in my wardrobe for myself, then we really do have a lot to discuss. Enjoy.'

'Talk to me,' Scarlet said. She was already pulling some knickers on.

'I've got to go, I really am busy.'

A running commentary about underwear with Scarlet he really did not need!

It felt odd to be out in the village. Scarlet had found a scarf and wrapped it around her head. Not so much to hide, but she didn't get why everyone was saying it was mild for November. She'd never felt more frozen in her life.

One thing the English did very well, though, Scarlet decided as she walked through the store, was cookies! Then she saw a recipe card for coffee-and-walnut cake and decided that she'd make that and bought the necessary ingredients. Happy with her purchases, she headed out of the shop but then caught sight of her reflection.

She looked like the Matchstick Girl in the clothes Luke had bought her so she walked into a small boutique and smiled at a woman behind the counter.

'Hi,' Scarlet said.

'Hello!'

She started to look through the racks of clothing. 'Are you looking for something special?' the woman asked.

'I'm looking for something not too special.' Scarlet sighed. 'I'm staying with a friend and I don't have much with me.'

Her name was Margaret and she was lovely and a happy hour was spent trying on various pieces of clothing. Scarlet had soon amassed quite a collection.

'Ooh, I haven't seen this one,' Margaret said, as Scarlet handed over her card to pay.

That card and the money on it was Scarlet's biggest achievement, not that Margaret could know. It had taken a year to get to this point. A year of squirrelling away cash, pretending she wanted to know what it felt like to go into a restaurant and pay. Setting up an account on an auction sight and selling signed photos. Just putting a little away with a dream in mind.

And maybe that dream had been a cottage on the beach to clear her head before she again faced Luke, but that hadn't quite worked out. Still, it felt brilliant to choose and buy her own clothes.

It was a very different house that Luke came home to—the scent of cake hit him as he came in and there was Scarlet looking like a Scarlet he had never seen.

Gone the celebrity, gone too the Matchstick Girl clothes he had inadvertently bought her.

She was wearing a huge chunky nutmeg jumper and thick black stockings and black velvet stilettos and, possibly, a skirt, but the jumper was a bit too big to tell.

'Wow,' Luke said.

'I know.' Scarlet grinned as she spread icing. 'It's my first cake.'

He wasn't talking about the cake but he made the right

noises, even if it did look like she was icing two burnt pancakes.

'How's Mom?'

'They're going to try and take off the ventilator later on today.'

'Should I be there?'

'She's going to be drowsy at first...'

'Luke, please, tell me what to do.'

'Whatever it is that you want to do,' Luke said. 'Scarlet...' He wanted her away from that woman, and to never have to see her again.

But it wasn't his place to say that.

She busied herself icing her cake.

'Coffee and walnut,' Scarlet explained.

They were pecan nuts but he chose not to say anything.

He put a finger in the icing mix and it was butter and not much else.

'It doesn't look like the picture.' Scarlet sighed.

'They never do.'

'I hope they like it.'

'Who?' Luke said, and then realised she had made it for his parents' visit. He'd actually forgotten they were coming. The whole drive home he'd been thinking about Scarlet and her mother, interspersed with Scarlet and what knickers she was wearing.

'Look, I know my being here might make things awkward for you, so if you don't want to have to explain me I can go for a walk.'

'I don't explain myself to my parents,' Luke said. 'The same way they don't have to explain themselves to me.'

'I just don't want to create tension.'

'Oh, there'll be tension,' Luke assured her, 'but I promise it has nothing to do with you. There's no need to be nervous.'

'Easy for you to say. Do they know about us, about…?'

Luke shook his head and gave a tense shrug. 'A bit.'

'How much?'

'Just that I met you a couple of years ago. Marcus wouldn't stop going on about it. They don't know the other stuff.'

'Do they work?'

Luke nodded. 'My father's a professor in cardiology.'

'Your mother?'

'She's a curator.'

He looked at her and could see she was daunted, so he came over and wrapped his arms around her waist. 'Just be yourself.'

'Sure.'

'Scarlet…' He looked right into her navy eyes and, yes, he loathed sharing but he loathed her unease with herself even more, so he said what he could to help her relax. 'My father screws around like you wouldn't believe. He has affair after affair. Some casual, which my mother ignores. Sometimes they get serious and my mother hits the gin when it does.'

Scarlet just looked at Luke as he gave a weary sigh and told her some more.

'Then he stops seeing his mistress, my mother stops drinking, everyone's happy and the cycle repeats itself. It's like living in the laundromat.'

Scarlet laughed. 'How do you know?'

'It's obvious. Well, it is to me but, with that said, Marcus and Emma don't have a clue…'

'Emma?'

'My sister.'

'Oh, I thought she was a lady friend.'

'You're my lady friend,' Luke said, and then he changed tack because his hands were moving southwards. 'Anyway, this weekend they're going to be celebrating thirty-two years of dysfunction, but I'm not allowed to say that.'

She frowned.

'I'll raise a cup of tea and we'll have some walnut cake that you very nicely made and they'll carry on their way. And no doubt by Sunday he'll be out with his latest and my mother will be passed out on the sofa.'

'Why are you telling me this?'

'Because I don't want you to feel intimated.' Luke let out a breath and Scarlet looked at this very deep man.

'Thank you.'

'For?'

'Telling me,' Scarlet said, and then she smiled. 'Some of it.'

He smiled back and then he stopped smiling as tears filled her eyes.

'I'm scared about my mom...'

'I know. Look, I've taken tomorrow off—' Luke started, then groaned when he heard a car in his driveway. 'They're here.'

Oh, they were, and they were also very taken aback to find Scarlet in situ.

Thankfully, though, it would seem they cared less about the famous Anya than they did about their son. His mother ran a very disapproving eye over Scarlet's stockinged legs and the questionable presence of a skirt, and his father simply looked her up and down.

Oh, my God, Scarlet realised, James Edwards was seriously checking her out.

Scarlet actually wanted to laugh as she saw Luke's eyes briefly shutter.

'You made cake!' Rose Edwards spoke as if Scarlet had just come in from the fields and mastered the appliances.

Which she sort of had!

'Not too much,' Rose said, as Scarlet cut a very generous piece.

'So, do you work at the Royal?' James asked her legs as she handed him a plate.

'No.' Scarlet smiled. 'I'm taking a break at the moment.'

'Studying?' Rose checked.

'No.' Scarlet gave Luke a slice. 'I'm just—'

'Scarlet's just taking some time out,' Luke said, and watched his mother pull a noncomprehending face and give a little shrug in a way only Rose could.

'Luke didn't mention anything,' Rose said, and then she frowned. 'Scarlet? Weren't you two…?'

'Scarlet and I go back a couple of years.' Luke gave nothing away with his response. 'She's over from LA and has come to stay for a few days.'

The cake really was amazing! Burnt and unrisen and the butter cream was almost pure butter.

'You're not having any?' Rose said to Scarlet as they all chewed through hell.

'Oh, no.' Scarlet screwed up her nose. 'Full of carbs!'

Luke actually laughed and never had he been more grateful for poor cooking skills because when Scarlet went to offer more, his mother pointed out they had to be in London by seven.

'Can't count on the traffic,' James said.

Scarlet said her goodbyes but stayed in the kitchen because Rose was making frantic eye gestures to Luke to have a word outside.

'Has she moved in?' Rose demanded.

'Temporarily, yes,' Luke replied.

'Luke, she's…' Rose was all pursed lips. 'Just watch yourself.'

Luke stood as they drove off and his father took another brick out of his wall. He walked inside.

'Is that American hussy after your money?' Scarlet was sitting on the kitchen bench and grinned as he walked back into the kitchen.

'It would seem so.'

'Your father!' Scarlet started laughing. 'He spoke to my thighs.'

'I don't know what to say about that.' What could he say? 'Never let him give you a tour of the library.'

'Well, if I ever do get to see your home I'll bear that in mind.'

He came over and she wrapped her arms around his neck, and she could just feel his tension. She just looked at him and smiled.

'Are you adopted?' she teased, only because Luke was a younger version of his father but their personalities could not be more different.

'I wish.'

'Is he like that with all your...?' She hesitated. She wasn't really a girlfriend, she was just the hot mess that had landed at his door.

'Yep,' Luke said. 'So don't take it as a compliment.'

'I shan't.'

He looked at her and usually he found family occasions, particularly if there was a girlfriend present, excruciating, but this one had almost ended with a smile.

His father's actions reflected no more on him with Scarlet than Anya's did on her. Still, he was cross with them.

'I can't stand how she doesn't notice what he's up to, or pretends not to,' Luke said. 'And yet she nitpicks and judges everyone, what they wear, how they talk...'

'How they cook...' Scarlet smiled. 'Poor Luke, having to eat that awful cake!'

'I like it,' Luke said.

'Good, because it's dinner.'

Now she did make him smile. What he had said before about Scarlet clearing his head was true. It was as if the rest of the world was crazy when it was just the two of them.

'You look beautiful,' Luke said.

'I went shopping.'

'I can see.'

'And I *love* my presents.'

'I want to see.' He ran a hand over her bottom as she sat on the bench and they kissed. A kiss that both had been waiting for. Her hands pressed into his hair and Luke moved in between her thighs and she wrapped them around his waist.

His kiss deepened, as if making up for two years of none. A slow, deep kiss that she didn't want to end but it did.

Luke remembered how upset she had been just before his parents had arrived.

He didn't want this to be about distraction. Both knew that at any moment the phone would go and there would be news about her mother. And, though he wanted more than anything to take her up to bed, or even on the kitchen table, there was so much to sort out first.

'Do you want to go and visit your mum?'

'You don't want to drive all that way again…'

'Do you want to go in?' he offered again.

'I don't know.'

'That's an answer,' Luke said. 'It's okay not to know.'

They went through to the lounge and it was like waiting for a bomb to go off. Scarlet sat cross-legged, tapping one foot, and then came over and lay on the coach, in her favourite spot—her head on his lap.

'I can take you in tomorrow and I can stay with you while you speak with her.'

'There's no need for that.' Scarlet shook her head. 'I know you think she's awful but she's not all bad...'

'No one is,' Luke said. 'It would be so much easier if that were the case.'

'She can be so nice. I don't know how to tell her I'm leaving after she's been so ill.'

'Leaving's hard,' Luke said. 'Even when there's no real reason to. Especially when there's no real reason.' And he told her a bit about the demise of his relationships prior to her. 'It's hard to admit something's not working when there's nothing really wrong, but sometimes...'

'What?'

'Well, you should *want* to stay,' Luke offered, not just to Scarlet but to himself as he thought of the demise of too many okay-ish relationships. 'Not have to come up with reasons to.'

He picked up his phone to glance at the time and Scarlet took it as a sign he was about to get up so she turned in his lap. 'Don't go...' She ran a hand over him and her lips did the same. Luke took her hand as she went for his zipper.

'I wasn't going anywhere,' Luke said.

'Just making sure...'

'Scarlet, I don't need a blow job to stay on the couch with you.'

He watched her face redden and tears fill her eyes, but he wasn't shaming her, more those who had taught her that was the way to make someone stay.

'You don't want me.'

'I want *you*.'

'And I want you to hold me.'

Finally!

He lay down beside her and showed her how nice it was to be held for no reason other than that.

'You're hard,' Scarlet said a little while later.

'It'll pass.' Luke grinned. He was as turned on as hell but there was a reason he wasn't tearing her clothes off now and he stopped smiling. 'Is that how you get your affection, Scarlet?'

He'd guessed as much but it hurt when she nodded.

They needed to start from the beginning, and that was why they lay there, half talking then dozing, and he wished they could stay there, but time moved quickly when you didn't want it to and just as Scarlet dozed off he heard the buzz of his phone.

He took the phone call and then sat there quietly for a moment and looked down at Scarlet. He did not want to invade her peace.

But he had to.

'Scarlet…'

'Mmm…'

'That was Craig, the anaesthetist working this evening. It's okay…' He felt her tense. 'Your mum's doing better.'

'Is she asking for me?'

'Yes.'

He could feel her rapid breathing.

'It wasn't an accident…'

'It was,' Scarlet said. 'She just took too much.'

'No.'

'It was.' She started to cry and Luke just sat there, thinking that her intense pain would stop soon because very soon it would be made to.

An accident.

Whoops.

But that just dulled the pain, it wouldn't take it away.

'I need to see her.'

'She's very angry and upset,' he warned, but Scarlet was already pulling on her shoes and he had this awful feeling that back to her world she was going. Especially when she went upstairs and started filling her bag with her flats and the scarf she had pinched from him.

He stood in the doorway, watching her, and told himself that they had, from the moment they had met, been temporary.

'Can I have my clothes,' Scarlet said, 'and my phone?'

'Are you coming back here?' Luke asked.

She just looked at him. 'I don't know!'

Her honest answer felt like she'd thrown a knife.

Luke's eyes felt as if he'd been swimming underwater as he drove back in to work.

People were right—he should live closer.

Except, as he looked over at Scarlet, he wouldn't change where he lived for the world. At least she'd had some time away. He just wished he could have given some more.

He had called ahead before he'd left and had spoken with Lorna, who was back for her night shift.

'David should be in soon,' Lorna said.

'It's not David I'm ringing for,' Luke said. 'Lorna, I'm bringing Anya's daughter in. Could we use the direct theatre lift?'

There was a very long pause as Lorna resisted asking any questions. 'Of course,' she said. 'Do you know the code?'

'I do.'

'I'll see you shortly, then.'

His filthy Audi moved unnoticed into the car park and they took the elevator up to the ground floor, where they headed straight to the central column.

There they took the service lift straight up to Theatre and then another up to ICU. Instead of arriving in the corridor, as the other elevators did, they stepped straight onto the ward.

To their credit, the staff there gave him no more than a slight wide-eyed look as Luke came over to the desk with Scarlet.

'Hi, Scarlet.' Lorna smiled. 'Your mom's been asking after you.'

'I know.'

'Why don't we go somewhere a little more private?' Lorna suggested, and glanced over at David, who nodded.

'I'll be there in a moment.'

'Do you want me to come with you?' Luke offered, but Scarlet shook her head so he stood there as Scarlet and Lorna headed off.

'I'm not sure what's going on between you two,' David said, 'and I don't need to know.'

'Thanks.

'You need to know this, though,' David said. 'She's about to walk into the lion's den.'

'I know she is.

Scarlet sat and listened to Lorna, who explained that her mother was doing a lot better but was insisting that she be moved elsewhere. 'She's not being very cooperative,' Lorna explained gently. 'And she's also extremely angry.'

'With me?'

'With everyone,' David said as he walked in, and Lorna looked up and smiled. 'I want her to stay here and I've told her that but she wants to be moved. I've told her that can't happen yet.' He was honest with Scarlet. 'I've dragged out a couple of procedures and told her it wasn't possible till late tomorrow but I can't force her to stay.'

Scarlet nodded. 'I know.'

'She's very insistent that she leaves.'

'Anya can be exceptionally difficult,' Scarlet said. 'I'm very sorry—'

'Scarlet,' David interrupted, 'you have nothing to apologise for.'

And she took a breath because she knew he wasn't just telling her that she didn't need to apologise for her mother's behaviour tonight.

This wasn't her fault.

Scarlet told herself that as she stepped behind the curtains and saw her mother lying there.

Lorna stayed with her but it wasn't pretty.

It was her fault apparently, and basically Anya told her that if at first she didn't succeed then she would try and try and try again because she could not live without her daughter by her side.

Luke had always thought that he was the strong one.

It had been an assumption of his that was summarily squashed when, after a few minutes of Anya's ranting, he heard Scarlet's clear voice.

'I'm going to go now, Mom. I love you. Please, get well.'

Scarlet walked out and straight to the elevator then she turned as if she'd forgotten something and thanked David. 'And can you thank Lorna?'

'Of course,' David said. 'Are you happy for me to call Luke with any change?'

'Please,' Scarlet said.

And that was it.

They stood in the elevator and made their way back to the underground car park, and Scarlet felt as if she might jump out of her skin.

'Can I drive?' Scarlet said suddenly.

'Of course.' Luke handed her the keys and Scarlet climbed into the driver's seat.

'She blames you,' Scarlet said, 'well, when she's not blaming me.'

'I heard,' Luke said. He didn't really know what to say here but he tried. 'I'm sorry if I've caused a rift...'

'A rift?' She gave him a very wide-eyed look that told him he was a master of understatement and then turned her head to look over her shoulder as she reversed out. 'And do you really think any of this is your fault?'

Wisely he said nothing.

'What?' Scarlet challenged the silence. 'Why do you have to be responsible?'

'I'm not.'

'Why do I?'

'You're not.'

'No,' Scarlet said, and she briefly looked at him as they waited for the barrier to lift. 'I was always going to leave, Luke or no Luke.'

'It's left here,' Luke said, as she missed the exit.

'Not tonight it isn't.'

She drove out of the hospital as if they were being chased by the paparazzi and then he found out that, despite several prangs in her past, Scarlet could actually drive, and rather fast!

There was somewhere she needed to be. Scarlet had known it the very second Luke had broken the news to her.

It had been the place she'd intended to run to that awful morning and it was the place she was taking him now.

'Am I being kidnapped?' Luke grinned.

He didn't blame her in the least for wanting a drive.

'Yep.' She looked over at him. 'So go to sleep. I don't want to talk.'

CHAPTER FOURTEEN

IT WAS A long drive, a very long drive through the night and she liked it that he didn't question her about where they were going and that after a while he slept.

God knew, he hadn't all week, Scarlet realised.

She read the signs, and the roads were very narrow and hilly, more so than she remembered. The hedges and stone walls loomed close but finally they had arrived and she pulled into a small deserted lookout and stared out at a waning moon and an angry black ocean.

The water looked a lot like she felt, cold and churned up and too dangerous to explore, but she wanted the man who was stretching out beside her to know her some more.

And so badly she wanted to know what went on in his head too.

Luke was so closed off and it had taken meeting his parents to realise that his guarded nature didn't just apply to her.

'Where the hell…?' Luke asked as he opened his eyes. The wipers were going full pelt but were still battling against the rain and the windscreen was fogging up.

'Devon,' Scarlet said.

Luke looked at the dashboard clock. It was five in the morning and pitch-black. The wind was howling, the sea was rolling black and white.

'I've dreamt about being here for a very long time.'

'Was it warm and sunny when you did?' Luke asked.

Scarlet shook her head. 'Nope.' It really was the place of her dreams but she had never dared to hope that she would ever be here with Luke.

They got out and Scarlet went into her bag and put on the horrible flat shoes he had bought her and then she put the giant bag over her shoulder. 'Leave it in the car,' Luke suggested, but Scarlet shook her head.

They didn't walk down to the beach, more the wind blew them onto it, and they ran hand in hand along the pebbly shore beside the roaring water.

Scarlet was angry, more angry and upset and terrified for her mother than she knew how to be, and Luke got that. He had heard her mother's cruel words and had seen Scarlet's calm exit but knew she was bleeding on the inside.

'I hate her. I love her but I hate her,' Scarlet said.

'Did you tell her that the other night?'

Scarlet nodded.

'You are allowed to say how you feel. What she did with that information was her choice.'

'You're allowed to say how you feel too,' Scarlet said, 'but you don't.'

'I know.' He pulled her right into his jacket and held her.

'What if she dies because I don't go back?'

And there was the reason that, in this, he didn't offer his thoughts, because one day that might well happen and he did not want to have influenced her choice.

He did not want, years from now, for there to be another reason for deep regret that came between them.

'If you do go back, will it change things?'

It was all he could offer and Scarlet tried to picture herself back home in LA and her mother well, simply because she was there by her side.

It hadn't worked so far.

For twenty-five years, being by her side hadn't worked.

'Do you know,' Luke said, and with his words he offered her no easy solution but acknowledged the hell her decision must be, 'with this wind, if you scream and face out to the water, no one will hear you?'

'Oh, they would,' Scarlet said, because the scream that she held inside was so loud it might split the channel they stared out at.

Luke shook his head. 'They won't.'

And so she did. Scarlet screamed and swore and kicked at the stones, and she was like the witches that she'd read flew over these parts, and it helped.

It really did.

And when her throat was as dry and as sore as it had been the morning she'd found her mother, the morning she had found Luke again, he took her in his arms and he held her.

They swayed to the sound of the waves and moved to their own tune, and against his chest the world felt better. With her in his arms, despite the darkness, the world seemed brighter.

And so they danced, and cared not if anyone was watching.

CHAPTER FIFTEEN

'LET'S GET BACK to the car,' Luke suggested.

Neither were dressed for the weather and both were frozen but Scarlet had other ideas and she took his hand and, shivering wet, gulping in cold air, she started walking along the beach.

With purpose.

They came to a small track and walked up it, arriving at a dark cottage. Luke frowned as she went into her bag and took out some keys. 'Scarlet?'

'I'm not breaking in.' Scarlet smiled through chattering lips. 'I want to show you something.' She pushed open the door and turned on a light, and Luke looked around and there, by the sofa, was a large bag.

'This is why I didn't get to see my mother go on stage that night.'

'What are you telling me, Scarlet?' Luke asked. 'Or, rather, what aren't you telling me?'

'A lot.'

There was a fire in the grate and she went to light a log with the matches provided, which didn't work, so he took some paper and scrunched it up beneath and kept feeding it till the log took.

And, because it was Scarlet, she stripped off, right down to her knickers, and Luke rolled his eyes but also stripped down. He couldn't be bothered to spread his clothes out so he threw them, suit and all, to shrink in the dryer and put a towel round his hips.

He didn't even bother to bring one for Scarlet.

She'd warmed some milk and made drinks and now sat by the fire. He went and sat beside her.

Luke was very used to asking patients their pain score from one to ten.

If there was such a thing as a want score, he'd be demanding knockout drugs now, because for all the times and opportunities they'd had to evade things with sex, this was the biggest challenge he'd met. But tomorrow her mother left and Scarlet might not be with her and he was here in the space she had fought for, in her terribly complex world.

She needed help, not his want.

'How long have you had this place?' Luke asked.

'I booked it a few weeks ago. I've been trying to leave for years,' Scarlet admitted. 'Since I was about fourteen. I just never knew how. I ran away when I was sixteen and I got as far as a bar.' She looked at him. 'I didn't know how to start, who to turn to,' Scarlet admitted. 'Then we had that night together and as terrible as things turned out I knew then that I had to do it. I started looking into ways when Mom said she was going back on tour. I've been squirrelling money away for this place. I've got it for a month. That's why I missed being there when she went on stage. I took a car the hotel provided and brought my stuff here.'

'Did your mum know?

'I told her that I wasn't going to be returning to America with her.'

'You could have got in touch with me, Scarlet. I'd have helped.'

'I know that you would have. I actually told Mom that

I would be looking you up, I thought it might be a bit of a false lead…'

That hurt but, Luke conceded, not as much as she was hurting right now so he let it slide.

'Even though I know what might happen to her, I'm not going back with Mom,' Scarlet said. 'I'm not cutting her out of my life for ever, but…'

She'd made her decision and had made it by herself, and instead of it hurting that she didn't need him, he was proud of the strongest woman he knew.

'I can't live like it any more. I've got this knot in my chest that I thought was normal until the night I spent with you. I honestly thought that was how life felt. I'm twenty-five, Luke. It shouldn't be called running away but that's what I feel like I'm doing to her…'

And he'd always held back. Luke had known she had to come to her own decision but he knew what a difficult one it must be for a woman who had never known anything other than the twisted love she'd been shown.

'You're not responsible for…' he attempted, and by reflex he felt her shoulders stiffen beneath his fingers. 'I've never run away,' Luke said. 'But I did skip school once.'

'Rebel,' Scarlet said, and her eye-roll suggested, what would he know?

'It was for me.' Luke smiled at her sulky expression. 'We took a train to London and went to the movies.'

'Did you get caught?'

'Sort of,' Luke said. 'Well, I ended up telling my mother…'

'You confessed!' Scarlet grinned. 'You are so damn…' And then she stopped because he just looked at her and he had told her something very few knew.

Not his brother or sister.

Nor his friends.

And certainly not girlfriends, because Luke's parents had warned him about sharing the truth.

'On the train back we were all fooling around and I looked over and I saw my father with a woman, getting off...'

Scarlet frowned.

They spoke the same language but it was so open to miscommunication that even Luke smiled. 'Not getting off the train, getting off with each other. Making out.'

'Did they see you?'

'No.' Luke shook his head. 'I went to another carriage and my friends followed. They never knew why I moved. I said I thought I'd seen an aunt.'

'You never said anything?' Scarlet checked, but then she knew she had said the wrong thing.

'Not at first. The next weekend I told my father that I'd seen him and that if he didn't tell my mother, I would.'

'And did he?'

Luke nodded.

'There were some terrible rows and after a couple of days he moved out. Marcus was about seven and Emma was five so they didn't really see it, but in the evenings my mother fell apart. She hit the bottle, cried her eyes out. One night I told her that she needed to go to bed. Do you know what she said?'

Scarlet just looked.

'This is all your fault.'

'For making your father tell her?' Scarlet checked, and Luke nodded.

'I realised then she hadn't wanted to know. I thought I was doing the right thing. I'd want to know, wouldn't you?'

'Oh, I'd know!' Scarlet said.

'She blamed it all on me. He did too. If I'd just shut up, none of that would have happened. After that I just stayed back. People can blow up their lives, do what they want. I'll fix them as much as they want to be fixed but I don't give unsolicited advice. Never again.'

She trusted him.

For the first time ever, she absolutely trusted another person.

Not more than she trusted herself, though.

He wasn't her safety net but it made the tightrope that she walked just a touch more steady.

'Can I ask you what you think I should do?'

Luke had held back for all the right reasons and for much better reasons he stepped in now.

'It isn't your fault. No matter what she says. It isn't. Change what you can,' Luke said, 'nurture the things that make you feel better. Follow your dreams and if that means you head to Africa...' He watched the reddening of her cheeks as he had one very special morning, and he'd been right—there were secrets in that pretty head. 'For what it's worth, I think you would be a brilliant midwife.'

It was worth so much.

'How can I be?'

She didn't feel she deserved it, Luke realised.

'Do you remember that nurse who was there for you? Was she perfect? I'll bet she didn't just sit with you, Scarlet. She brought some of her life, her experience to the bedside, and you've got a whole load of that.'

'Is that what you do?' She didn't get it, she just couldn't imagine Luke talking with someone and spilling out his life.

'In my own way,' Luke said. 'I don't jump in, I don't judge. It doesn't suit all my patients but for the ones that it does, they'll wait to see me.'

'I'd wait to see you.' Scarlet smiled. 'I used to think you were all like Vince.'

'Is that why you screwed your nose up when I said I was a doctor?'

Scarlet nodded. 'I hate that man so much. I was so happy when I found out that he'd only come on board when I was three. I used to worry that he was my father.'

'Do you know who your father is?'

'No idea,' Scarlet said. 'Nor does she.'

'Does it hurt, not knowing?'

'It used to,' Scarlet said. 'I had this notion that one day he'd come looking for me. By the time I got a bit older I'd worked out that, given my mother had no idea who it was…'

'I'm over casual sex,' Luke said, and he looked at her.

They were naked by a fire, the scene was set, he could have her now, but then again, Luke knew, she'd been so starved of affection that a burger could have got him there with Scarlet.

Not now.

She gave him a smile, she sat naked and looked at the most beautiful man on earth and she felt on the edge of something, that love really was worth holding out for.

'And me.'

CHAPTER SIXTEEN

'I DON'T KNOW if I should try and speak with her one more time,' Scarlet said

Luke was driving, and they were near the turn off that decided if they headed for home or the hospital.

He was honest.

'I think you have to,' Luke said. Even if just for Scarlet's sake, maybe it was better that she try again, but Scarlet shook her head.

She knew just how poisonous her mother could be.

It had taken the time away to see it.

'I can speak with her if you want.'

'You?'

'Well, she did ask me to be her doctor once.'

'I thought you stayed back?'

'Not in this.'

There were press everywhere. News of Anya's impending transfer had leaked, but not by the staff at the hospital, Luke knew that.

He nodded to Geoff, who gave him the most bored shrug as he gestured Luke's car to turn to the right. And Luke would thank him later for not letting on that a valuable photo was sitting with her heavy head leaning against the window of his car.

He parked and, at Scarlet's request, he left her in the car. On his way to ICU he called Angie.

He gave sparse details. It was for Angie to make her own judgements and he did all he could not to cloud them.

'If you could be there when I speak with Anya...'

'What if she agrees that I take her on?' Angie checked. 'I'm serious, Luke. If she's my patient...'

'I'll never ask,' Luke said. 'And I'm not just talking professionally, I'd never jeopardise our friendship.'

Absolutely he knew the value of a real friend who wasn't paid for, one who didn't simply say the right thing because it might be easier to hear a lie than the truth.

'Well, make sure you don't,' Angie said. 'I'll meet you up there.'

'Anya's about to be transferred,' David said when Luke came into the ICU.

'To?' Luke checked, and was informed that Anya was being transferred to a very swish private hospital for a couple of days and then would be heading for home.

'She wants her daughter.' David rolled his eyes. 'And she's not used to not getting what she wants.' He glanced over at the close curtains. 'She's furious that she isn't in a private room. She has no concept of ICU.'

'Can I speak to her?'

'You know you can.' David nodded. 'Though I have to say I don't think a lecture from the doctor who resuscitated her is going to do much. Still, it's worth a try.'

'Oh, no.' Luke was honest. 'I'm not here for that. I was invited to be her private doctor once.'

'You!' David frowned and then grinned. 'You?' he checked again.

'Yep, me,' Luke said. 'And, as you've probably guessed, her daughter is staying with me.'

'We had kind of worked that out, long before you brought her up here.'

'How?' Luke asked, not worried that they had, just curious to know.

'Well, the car Scarlet arrived in, Geoff kind of recognised, so we checked her emergency contact phone number and it matched yours.' David grinned. 'Talk about a dark horse…' As Angie came over and joined them, David stopped smiling and shook his head. 'I can tell you now, Angie, that she's certainly not going to speak with you.'

'Well, let's just give Anya that choice,' Angie said, and Luke watched as his friend and ex-lover put her psychiatrist's hat on firmly.

'Are you going to come in?' Luke asked David. 'I'd prefer you to hear what's said.'

'Sure.'

They all walked over and Luke took a breath and then parted the curtain.

'Anya…' He gave her a thin smile. 'I'm Luke Edwards…'

Anya just stared.

'I was the consultant on duty in Emergency when you came in.'

'And I want to thank you.' Anya said.

'There's no need.'

'Oh, but there is.' She reached for his hands and, Luke thought, for all the agony she had caused her daughter, she didn't even remember his name.

'You invited me to be your private doctor a couple of years ago…'

'Excuse me?'

'Your daughter was pregnant and you wanted to put me on your payroll,' Luke said, and he watched as Anya blinked. 'But I refused.'

'I don't want to talk about that time.'

'It's a very painful topic, I agree,' Luke said, 'and as difficult as it might be to do so, it's better that it's discussed.'

'Have you got my daughter?'

'*Got* your daughter?' Luke checked. 'Yes, Scarlet has been staying with me, and before you press that call bell, I want you to listen to me.'

'Well, I don't want to.'

'I'm going to say what I've come to and then I'm going to go.' He introduced Angie and said that she was a psychiatrist who specialised in addiction.

'Oh, please...' Anya said. 'Is this an intervention?'

'Minus the cameras.' Luke nodded. 'Anya, we're extremely concerned. You attempted to take your life and very nearly succeeded...'

'I told the nurse this morning that I was confused when I said that last night. It was an accident.'

'Anya.' Luke held out her drug screen but she refused to take it. 'I cannot see how this could be an accident but if it somehow was, then how that happened needs to be addressed.'

'Which is why I'm being transferred,' Anya said. 'Where's Scarlet?' she demanded, and started shouting for her daughter. 'You're to bring her to me.'

'I'm going to take care of your daughter for as long as she wants me to,' Luke said. 'Me. No bodyguards, no cameras, and if you tell your crew where she is, or it comes out, you are to tell them that they are not to come. If I see another car in the street or someone at my door, I'll move on with Scarlet for as long as she wants to. I will never live your life.'

'You regret it,' Anya sneered. 'If you'd been my doctor...'

'Oh, no,' Luke said. 'I look back on that time and, looking at your toxicology screen, I know for sure I could never have been your doctor. This woman should be,' Luke said, and Angie stepped forward. 'Stay here and work on yourself or go back to the world you've come from.'

'If she can leave her own mother,' Anya said, 'do you really think she's going to stick around with you and play the doctor's wife? She's using you.'

An escape route.

He'd thought about his friend's words at times.

And Scarlet had said herself that she'd used him as a false lead.

But his love was real.

And if that meant he was an escape route, Luke could live with that.

Scarlet's future was worth it.

'We're different people, Anya.' He looked down at her. 'I believe that when you love someone, their happiness becomes a priority. I don't want Scarlet trapped and miserable. She's not some toy for me to keep locked away in the hope she won't leave.' And once, just once, calm, professional and detached he could not be because he sneered at her. 'As you've found out, it doesn't work.' He headed for the curtain and then he turned around. 'There is one thing you don't have to worry about, though—whatever she needs, I'll always be there for Scarlet.'

CHAPTER SEVENTEEN

'WHAT DID SHE SAY?'

Luke sat in the car beside Scarlet and even as he'd climbed in, it felt as if her mother's shadow had got in with him.

'Not much,' Luke said. 'Angie's in with her now.'

She looked at him. 'I don't believe you,' Scarlet said, and saw the set of his jaw. 'Tell me what she said.'

'Just...' Anya's words buzzed in his head. They were a touch too close to home but he did his best to ignore them. 'She was never just going to lie back and let you go. It doesn't matter what she said.'

Scarlet sat there and was glad that Luke didn't turn on the engine but just let her sit with her thoughts.

'I can't just leave her.'

'Scarlet,' Luke said. 'I think that even if you go back with your mother, nothing will change. I don't think anything you do can alter that fact.'

'I know that.'

'But if you feel you have to go back, I get that.'

'What about us?'

It wasn't a selfish question and it was one Luke pondered for a moment before answering. They had been together again for only four days and before that it had been just one night.

'You've still got my phone number?' Luke checked.

Scarlet nodded.

'We're thirty-fifteen on hanging up on each other. It's your turn next.'

'We'll talk?'

'Every morning and every night, just as much as you want to,' Luke said. He hadn't been lying to Anya. He would be there for Scarlet for as long she needed him to be. 'And I've got leave I can take so I can get on a plane and so can you.'

'Are we just friends?'

'In this,' Luke answered carefully, 'I'm your *best* friend. I promise you that, Scarlet. You do what you have to do.'

He gave her the one thing she'd never had—options.

Precious, rare options that came with no strings attached.

No want, or need, to drag her back, no promise of all he could do for her, no safety net, yet he made her able to fly.

'I'm going to go and speak to her,' Scarlet said. Luke was right, for that she *needed* a friend. 'Can you come up with me?'

'Of course.'

Luke walked with her right up to the unit and then he saw Angie coming out from behind the curtains.

'Hi, Midwife Lucy.' Angie smiled and then, when Scarlet felt she might break, Angie gave her a hug. 'It's okay.' Angie gave Luke a smile and then dismissed him. 'I'm going to speak with Scarlet.'

Scarlet sat in another interview room, where she guessed that people were told their loved ones had died. But then she thought about Evan, finding out that his son had a stab at life, and this was a bittersweet room she found herself in, Scarlet decided as Angie went through things with her.

It was just more of the same.

'Your mum insists on leaving here tonight,' Angie concluded. 'She's coherent, she knows what she wants…'

'So do I,' Scarlet said. She did now. 'Can I see her?'

'Of course you can.' Angie nodded.

She had choices and so did her mom.

'Please, take the help that's being offered,' Scarlet said as she sat at her mother's bedside.

'I don't need their help. It was an accident.'

And back to lying and blackmailing Anya went. 'I was thinking, in a few weeks you could go to Africa. I know you love going there and maybe—'

'I'm not coming back with you, Mom.'

'You're going with him,' Anya sneered. 'Believe me, Scarlet, you're only as good as your last—'

'Don't you dare!' Scarlet stood. She just stood up then and she thought of a man who had said no to her frequent offers, and if it had confused her at times it all made beautiful sense now. She could look her mother in the eye and know absolutely that what she said was right. 'I count for so much more than that with him.'

'Please,' Anya sneered. 'Is that what he told you?'

'That's what he *showed* me,' Scarlet said, and tears filled her eyes because over and over, every step of the way, Luke had. 'You need help, Mom.'

'I don't need help.'

'Well, I do,' Scarlet said. 'I need friends, I need support and I need space. I want a career, Mom. You've got one…'

It was almost pointless, but not quite. She was allowed to have hope that one day her mum would be well.

Not yet, though.

She kissed her mum goodbye, even if it wasn't returned, and then walked out and said thanks to Angie, who was sitting at the desk with Luke.

'This way,' Scarlet said to him, and instead of leaving via the internal lift they headed towards the main exit.

There were many reasons to be proud of her, Luke thought, because as they passed Ashleigh's bed, where he lay with his headphones on, Ashleigh gave his father a nudge as Scarlet walked past.

'Not now,' Evan said to his son. Curtains were thin and he'd heard what had just gone on.

Yes, now, Scarlet thought.

And Luke saw first-hand the absolute star that Scarlet was.

'Hey!' Scarlet smiled at Ashleigh and went over. 'Wow! You are looking so much better.'

'I'm feeling it,' Ashleigh admitted. 'I'm going to a regular ward tomorrow.'

'That's brilliant.' Scarlet smiled. 'Do you want a photo of the two of us?'

'Are you sure?'

'Of course I am.'

They snapped a photo, one that caught Scarlet kissing him on the cheek, and Ashleigh grinned as he looked at it. 'I won't share it.'

'Go for it.' Scarlet smiled. 'Show the world how much better you're doing and that they need to watch out.'

She was speaking for both of them!

They didn't leave by the lifts; instead, they walked out the regular exit and Scarlet asked, in no uncertain terms, for Sonia to hand over her passport.

'It's back at the hotel.'

'Then go and fetch it,' Scarlet said, and took a seat. 'I'll wait.'

'Actually...'

Surprise, surprise, Sonia had it in her bag.

And that was it, she was free.

They drove home in silence at first and Scarlet rested her head on the window.

'Thank you,' Scarlet said.

'For what?'

For being the true friend she'd never had. 'All that you've done for me. I've completely messed up your week.'

Luke swallowed. She hadn't messed up his week, she had changed his entire life, but that might not be what she needed to hear now.

'Do you know what you want to do?'

'Do?' Scarlet frowned. 'I don't know. Maybe...' she took a breath '...go to the cottage perhaps, do what I planned to and get my head together.' She took a breath. 'You'll get sick of me soon...'

Luke frowned.

'Tired of my dramas.'

'That's what she said,' Luke pointed out, because, yes, curtains were thin.

Luke looked at the road ahead.

Ten minutes in that woman's company and Anya had watered the weeds of doubt in both of them.

He had never admired Scarlet more—she'd had a lifetime of it but instead of weeds the flowers had somehow thrived.

And the lunatics were not running the asylum, Luke decided.

He was.

If what he had to reveal to Scarlet was too much, too soon, and not what she needed or wanted, then so be it, he wouldn't crowd her.

But something told him that what he felt inside was right. That his words were something that Scarlet, who had never properly been loved, maybe needed to hear.

Whatever she did with that knowledge was fine with Luke but she deserved to know just how very loved she was.

It was time to do what he avoided.

Tell another person just how he felt.

CHAPTER EIGHTEEN

THEY DIDN'T PULL into his house; instead, they pulled up outside the pub.

'What are we doing?'

'Well, I don't feel like cooking, do you?'

'No!' Scarlet admitted.

'So let's have dinner here.'

They walked in together and Scarlet was more nervous than she'd been when she'd stepped on stage in Paris and had had her mother sing to her, but Luke was calm and relaxed.

'Hi, Luke,' Von, the landlady, said.

As they sat down a young couple did a double take and when one of them picked up their phone and started to walk over, Trefor, who was in with his wife, stopped them and reminded them that her mother was terribly ill.

They sat back down and the phone went back on the table.

Scarlet gave them a wave. 'Hi, Margaret.'

'It's lovely to see you, Scarlet.'

They took a seat and Luke grinned.

'What?' Scarlet checked.

'She bought me a casserole the day I moved in. I was so taken aback I forgot her name and for months I've been trying to find it out, without admitting I don't know.'

'Margaret,' Scarlet said. 'The shop's not doing too well, she's thinking of making a web page.'

'You chatted?'

'She helped me choose my outfit,' Scarlet explained.

'And she chose your knickers too,' Luke pointed out.

'I thought you chose them.' Scarlet smiled but she was frowning a little because that little comment was so open to one of her more usual responses, and Luke didn't generally offer such openings.

'I thought it safer to leave it to her,' Luke admitted.

'Safer?' Scarlet checked.

'That you were dressed by Margaret.'

She wanted to be undressed by Luke, though.

'You're in an odd mood,' Scarlet commented.

'Doesn't feel odd to me,' Luke said, and she looked at him, grateful that now she could do just that.

He smiled at her, not a grin or a happy smile, just a knowing one that had her toes curl in her shoes because she wanted to reach over and tell him she was wearing the purple knickers.

She restrained herself.

The shadow that had followed them since they had been to the hospital had lifted but the clearer air between them slightly dizzied her.

She was nervous to provoke, worried she was misreading the edge they were on.

God! Scarlet just sat there and went bright red with recall at some of the offers she'd made so readily, assuming that was what it took to be a guest in his home.

Luke gestured to a chalkboard. 'What do you want to eat?'

Scarlet screwed up her noise as she read the choices.

'The steak and kidney pie is good here,' Luke suggested.

She made a gagging face.

'Really good,' Luke said, unimpressed.

'Fine, then,' Scarlet said, and looked around for someone to take their order. 'Where are you going?'

'To order.' Luke disappeared and she sat there as he did so.

And still she sat there as he went over and had a quick word with Margaret and Trefor and then after a while he came back with two little bottles and two glasses.

'What are these?'

'Grapefruit juice for you,' Luke said, as he poured them. 'And pineapple juice for me.'

And she went a bit pink and then asked a question. 'Why do you have grapefruit juice in your fridge when you don't like it?'

She was so clever, so astute, Luke thought, and he wondered about all she could be.

'I have it in my fridge because I drink it every morning and think of you for a couple of minutes.'

'Oh, so you drink something you don't like and think of me...'

'I love it now,' Luke said. 'That time in the morning that I spend thinking of you is both the worst and best part of my day.'

She just looked at him, into those beautiful eyes, and love hurt so much more than she had ever thought it might.

'You think about me every day?'

'All day,' Luke said.

'And the trouble I make?'

'I think about so much more than that.' He took a breath. 'You know that there have been others—'

'Luke,' Scarlet interrupted. 'I don't want to hear about them. I know we need to talk but I can't take it today.'

'Yes, you can,' Luke said. 'I want to tell you something, I want you to know that, while there might have been others, I've never had sex in the morning since you. And do you know what else? I don't even have breakfast in bed any more, and if I'm in a hotel I go down and eat at the buffet.'

'Why?'

'I want to have that breakfast in bed with you.'

He just stared at her and she said nothing and then their plates came and she picked out all the kidney and tackled the rest of the pie.

'It's yum,' she conceded, glad of the diversion because talking today was surely too hard. She tried to keep it light as she turned her attention to the pastry.

Once she had finished her pie, she reached out to pick at his. 'You see, Luke, we really shouldn't be together because I'd be the size—'

'And I'd still want you,' Luke said, 'and if you stopped putting that stuff in your lips I'd want you even more.'

Scarlet looked at him. 'You say that now.' Her head was all jumbled and rather than look at him Scarlet had a piece of the kidney she'd picked out.

It was nice.

So nice that she had another piece.

And then she had another because if she didn't then she might open her mouth and tell him how much she loved him and beg him not to send her away now that her mum had gone.

Scarlet knew that she needed to get her head together; she wanted to be so suave and calm when she told him how she felt. 'I want to go to the cottage,' Scarlet said suddenly.

'I'll take you.'

'I want a few weeks to get my head together and then…'
He didn't rush in so she took a breath and told him what she'd been planning. 'I might call you once things are calmer. If that's okay?'

'Of course.'

'See how you're feeling about me then,' Scarlet said.

'It won't have changed,' Luke said. 'It hasn't in the two years that I've been hoping you might call.'

'You hoped I'd call?'

'Every day, and knowing you were in the country and hadn't...' Luke stopped, not wanting to lay a guilt trip on her. 'I can't see my feelings for you going away any time soon. At least, not in this lifetime. And if that's too much for you to handle, I get that...'

'Too much?' Scarlet checked. 'I thought you were just...'

'Just what?'

'Tolerating me.'

'I don't tolerate you, Scarlet, I love you.'

'What sort of love?' Scarlet checked. 'Like a sister?'

'I certainly hope not.'

'A fancy?'

'Much more than that,' Luke said. 'How about a real love, which, yes, I guess means I can tolerate anything if it helps you to get where you want to be. And if that means holing yourself up in a cottage, or flying off to Africa, or even going back to LA...'

'So long as there are no bodyguards?' Scarlet huffed.

'Scarlet, if you want to carry on as a celebrity, I'll work my way around it. I won't be giving tell-all interviews, though...' He smiled as she laughed at the very thought. 'And don't try sorting out my career for me again...'

'You'd come to LA?' Scarlet frowned. 'For me?'

'For us,' Luke corrected. 'You asked how the conversation would have been had you called, well...' He didn't finish; it still hurt that she hadn't.

It was Scarlet that spoke. 'I was going to call. I knew I'd made a mess of things last time and so I was going to try and work things out at the cottage. I wanted it all to be sorted and for me to be all...' She saw his smile. 'Well, a rather more sophisticated and together version of me was going to give you a call in a few weeks' time.'

She *had* been planning to call.

Their stars would have collided, Luke found out then, and he was no fool rushing in, this *was* love, he knew that now.

All the naysayers, all the doubters could leave now, please, Luke thought, because when it was just the two of them, all was right in the world.

He could tell her everything now.

'Come on,' Luke said.

As they walked out they stopped and chatted to *Margaret* and Trefor.

'I've got some new stock coming in next week,' Margaret said to Scarlet. 'You should come and have a look.'

'I shall,' Scarlet said.

As they walked out of the pub, Scarlet, a little distracted, holding Luke's words in her head and going over and over them, just so they wouldn't disappear, bumped into someone and turned.

And when she saw who it was Scarlet gaped.

'Come on, Scarlet,' Luke said, and grabbed her by the hand as she craned her neck for another look. 'It's rude to stare.'

'But isn't that…?' Oh, my God, she knew that couple— the whole world did.

'Yes,' Luke said. 'They're even more famous than you.'

They walked out of the pub and there was his car.

'I can take you to the cottage now,' Luke said, dangling his keys. 'You can go and get yourself all suave and sophisticated if you want to…' he offered, and she poked out her tongue.

'I can't leave yet.' Scarlet shook her head and they walked hand in hand towards his home. 'I said I'd go and help Margaret get her store online on Monday. Apparently men feel very awkward when they come in to buy things.'

'I don't think so.'

'And they're not very knowledgeable,' Scarlet said. 'I'm not a size *small*, Luke,' Scarlet said and she told him her size. 'Just for future reference.'

Their future was referenced and that made them both smile.

But then Scarlet stopped smiling and she thought of all that had been lost, all the damage done.

'Can we ever get past it?' Scarlet said, and they stopped walking and faced each other.

'We have to get through it,' Luke said. 'And we *can* get through it together.'

They shared a soft kiss that tasted of regret mingled with love as they shared the hurt and what could have been and what had been lost.

They would work through it together.

He smelt her hair and she just leant against him. It was gone.

Her shame.

His acceptance of her, good, bad and the middle bits, would not allow shame to reside in her.

They walked to the house that had a few missing bricks in the driveway wall and she waited for Luke to open the door.

'You've got a key,' Luke said. 'Scarlet, this is your home.'

'Mine.' She laughed at the very notion but then she found out just how much he loved her.

'This village is why I live so far from work. There are couples here who are just as high profile as you are, more so, and they get to live a very normal life on their days off. They might have to work at it, but when they do...'

'You chose this house with me in mind?'

'Everything has been with you in mind. And if that's too much...'

'Too much? No. Never.'

She could never get enough of his love.

'So open up and let us in,' Luke said.

Scarlet did. She turned the key to her home and they both stepped in, and they would keep opening up and keep letting the other in every day of their lives, both swore.

She stood in the hall and resisted the urge to snap a photo and post it and share her joy with the world, but she was very easily distracted by Luke.

'What are you doing?' Scarlet asked. He began to strip off her clothes. 'Luke...'

'What I've been wanting to do all along.'

CHAPTER NINETEEN

'I LOVE YOU.' Luke told her the truth and it came from the very bottom of his heart. 'I have loved you from the moment I saw you.'

It made perfect sense now.

Love had led them to now.

'I love you back,' Scarlet said, and she wasn't afraid to admit it now. Furthermore, there was no hope of being sophisticated and level-headed when Luke was close and holding her the way he was.

Two years after they'd found out that they did, they got to say it and could believe it now.

And this time when he carried her wriggling in his arms and she rained kisses on his face, he didn't deposit her on the spare bed but again Luke didn't pull back the sheets.

Deliberately this time.

He stared down at her as he undressed her in a way that had Scarlet squirm.

Off came that chunky jumper to reveal the very small purple bra. His hands went to unhook it and he removed it without a word.

Off came her shoes and that tiny, tiny skirt came down with her stockings.

'Luke…' Her hands reached out for him but he flicked them away.

He had waited, now so could she.

Scarlet lay as he peeled off her knickers so slowly that her breathing kept catching in her throat as she fought the temptation for haste. Then Luke stood and undressed himself and revealed that delicious male body again, though his eyes did not meet hers. He looked at that jet of hair that he'd tried so hard not to and his gaze burnt so much so that she just lay there and parted her legs.

Still he made her wait because he flipped her over onto her stomach and took her hands out from where they needed to be and placed them palms down beside her head.

He kissed her all over, from the nape of her neck to the soles of her feet. He kissed the small of her back and he kissed the cheek of her bottom so deeply that she started to sob with want. Then he turned her around and kissed her stomach with the same lavish attention. Her spine curved so that her hips lifted but Luke hadn't finished yet.

His fingers were inside her and stroking her as his mouth met her breast and tasted her again, and sucked and nipped till she was frenzied. When she could take it no more, he very abruptly removed his fingers, parted her legs and kissed inside her thighs, not tenderly but deep, bruising kisses that made her remember that a gentle lover he was not.

He tried to be.

But Luke forgot the gentleman he usually remembered to be when her scent hit him.

The silky black hair had not been there last time and Scarlet closed her eyes as his teeth nipped and tugged, and then came the heat his mouth delivered.

Every tear she had cried, all the pain of the days, the months and years dissolved as Luke probed her with his tongue. His hands parted her thighs farther when they tried to close in on his head. He completely exposed her, laved her, tasted her; he drew out musk, he tasted her deep and when she came he held her down and tasted her more, so she screamed.

As she tried to catch her breath he didn't allow her to; instead, Luke pulled her limp body up so she knelt and leant on his chest to recover. Very soon she did, stroking his thickness, feeling him again in her hands, wanting him, as she always had.

She left the safe haven of his chest and found his neck, and she bruised him now with her mouth as she raised herself, wanting him to gather her, yet he reached for the drawer.

'I want your babies…' Scarlet begged, not wanting to stop or wanting to part for a second.

'Not yet,' Luke said.

His love was older and wiser now and they would wait till they could cope with their love before adding to something so big, so precious and so worth protecting.

He opened the drawer and took out a condom and she took it from him and knelt back on her heels, stroking him with one hand and cupping his balls in the other until it was Luke who was now impatient.

'Scarlet…'

With aching slowness, she slid it on.

Luke pulled her in and they kissed, a sexy kiss, and she felt his tongue still and the holding of his breath as she slid down his length.

He moved her legs and they wrapped around him, and the feel of him filling her, moving in her while kissing her was sublime. Her lips closed and tightened and he forced them apart, and when his teeth gritted she felt him swell that final time and they gave up with mouths and just locked in eye contact for that final second before they were lost to each other.

His body mocked the times she had thought he might not want her as he thrust into her, so deep, and ground her down so hard that it could never now be questioned.

And one would hope there were no bodyguards outside the door, because she didn't hold back from sobbing or shouting, and as she came, tight around him, all his restraint was rewarded as he shot hard and released deep inside her.

And then they were back to the other, with eyes that stared right to the very bottom of the other's soul.

'What are you thinking?' Scarlet said.

'You don't want to know.'

'I do,' she persisted. 'Tell me.'

'That was an amazing come. I want to go again.'

'Just that?'

'Yep.'

'What else?' Scarlet smiled.

'I think I'm ready to go again.'

Still rivers did not run deeper when she was hot in his arms.

Scarlet laughed as they lay upside down in his bed. She then climbed up onto his stomach and sat there, playing with the hairs on his chest and loving that she was back where she belonged.

That they could talk now.

And for ever.

Luke loved it too. He looked up at her and she was lost to her thoughts. There were secrets inside that pretty head, he knew. 'What are you thinking?'

'Lots of things.'

'Like?'

'Have you really loved me all that time?'

She knew that he had, it was just hard to take in.

He reached out and opened the drawer, reaching not

for a condom this time but for a receipt, which he handed to her.

It was faded, a long bar bill, and on the end of it was a glass of champagne.

'I never keep mementos,' Luke said, 'but I just couldn't throw it out.'

And there was the hotel bill too and a serviette with faded lipstick, and he had loved her since then, absolutely she knew that.

'What else are you thinking?' Luke asked.

With his love, there were so many things to think about. 'All the things I can do.'

'Like?' He watched the blush on her cheeks.

'What you said about me being a midwife, did you mean it?'

'Absolutely,' Luke said. 'What else are you thinking?'

'That I want to get married.'

Both smiled.

'I would have got round to that,' Luke said.

'We'll be family then,' Scarlet said.

'You're my family now,' Luke told her, but he got her insecurity. 'We'll get married as quickly as I can arrange it.'

'I want a big ring,' Scarlet warned. 'I think it has to be a ruby, but a massive one.'

Luke rolled his eyes.

'And I want a church with bells and hymns and flowers...' Scarlet held nothing back with her demands. 'And I'm going to wear red and...' Then she looked at the most patient man in the world. 'I just want us there, though.'

'Oh, I think we can manage all that.' Luke smiled.

'Maybe Trefor and Margaret can be witnesses,' Scarlet mused.

'Perhaps a little drink back at the pub afterwards?' Luke suggested.

'And we could maybe have a teeny party there?' Scarlet checked. 'Just an impromptu one.'

'No wedding cake, then?' Luke checked.

'Oh, yes, I want cake.'

'You can have cake,' Luke said, 'just as long as you don't make it.'

'And I want wedding presents too.'

Ooh, it was going to take a lot of organising for their impromptu wedding!

His hands slid up from her waist to her breasts and she felt him nudging against the small of her back. She knew exactly what Luke was thinking now and it wasn't about weddings.

'I thought there was no hope for us,' Scarlet admitted.

'There's always hope.'

He believed that—all those years in Emergency had taught him.

Even when it seemed as if there was none.

It was almost impossible to fathom.

As she had been making her plans to escape, Luke had been creating a world she could run to.

And here she was.

In his bed, making love, planning weddings, getting on with their precious world.

That was love.

EPILOGUE

One year and eight months later

THIS WAS THE third birth she had witnessed as a student midwife.

Scarlet knew that she should, as the doctor had yesterday advised, be at home, putting her feet up, but she really wanted to finish this semester.

It was her second one and finally, after all these months of study, for two weeks she had been allowed in the maternity ward and these last two days had been spent in the delivery room.

'I can't do this,' Hannah said, and shook her head.

Hannah was eighteen and alone and terrified, and when she should really be down at the action end, instead Scarlet put her arms around the young woman's shoulders.

'You already are doing this,' Scarlet said.

They had a bond.

Scarlet's first day observing in the antenatal clinic had been Hannah's first visit some four months ago.

Hannah had asked loads of questions and Scarlet had admitted that it was her first day with a real patient and that soon the real midwife would be in and would answer those questions.

'Aren't you...?' Hannah had asked when she had read Scarlet's name tag.

It still happened.

The other day someone had said, 'Didn't you used to be Scarlet?'

'I'm still Scarlet...' she had smiled '...but, yes.'

And now here Hannah was, about to give birth.

Scarlet had arrived on the delivery ward that morning at eight.

A niggling back pain had woken her and had not relented as Luke had driven them into work.

By eight fifteen she had been about to make her excuses—her back had been killing her, the baby had felt as if it was between her thighs and she had known she was in labour. Scarlet had been about to go and find Luke when Hannah had said it.

'I want my mum.'

'I know that you do,' Scarlet said.

Sometimes, so too did Scarlet.

Yes, there had been terrible times but there had been happier ones too, and, as Luke had said, leaving was always hard.

Anya hadn't been able to make their not-very-low-key wedding.

It had been an amazing day. Luke's family had, of course, been invited, as well as David and Angie, who felt like her friends too.

And she had, of course, asked her mother.

Anya had said that she would come but had changed her mind at the last moment. She had called two days before the wedding and said that she was in the middle of recording and had people relying on her.

Scarlet had learnt not to.

Luke had tried to come up with a solution and had suggested that someone else give Scarlet away.

Only Scarlet didn't need anyone else.

'Who giveth this woman to marry this man?' the vicar had asked.

'I do,' Scarlet had said.

And on the day she had found out she was pregnant, she had sat on Luke's lap and cried both happy then sad tears. After a lot of thought she had decided not to call her mother just yet.

They had told no one for quite a while. Her pregnancy had been something that she and Luke had chosen not to share for as long as they had been able to keep it quiet.

They had held in their lovely secret and just taken their time to get their heads around it themselves.

Finally they would be parents.

Scarlet would soon be a mum, or a 'mom', as she called it.

Yes, sometimes you needed a mum or a mom but sometimes you had to make do, and for Hannah today that person was Scarlet.

'Don't leave me,' Hannah begged.

'I'm not going anywhere,' Scarlet replied.

'I can't do this,' Hannah said again.

'Yes, you can,' Scarlet promised, because when she looked down there was a head about to be delivered. 'Put your hands down,' Scarlet said, and guided them to the baby that was about to be born.

Scarlet was, as it turned out, very, very good with women at their most difficult and tumultuous times.

She'd had twenty-five years' experience with the most difficult of the lot, Scarlet had said when Beth, her mentor, had praised her on her ability to connect.

'One day it will be your turn,' Hannah shouted as she went to push again. 'Then you'll know how hard it is!'

Scarlet just held her shoulders and watched as Hannah's baby was delivered onto her stomach and all was quiet with the world except for the noise of a newborn's cries.

A beautiful little boy, who was actually a very big boy, Scarlet thought as she put a little name band on his fat wrists.

And then another contraction came.

Hannah was right. Soon *she* would know.

Very soon, Scarlet thought as her stomach tightened for what seemed a very long time. And, no, these were definitely not imaginary pains and neither were they going away.

'Are you okay, Scarlet?' Beth checked, after they had helped Hannah into a fresh bed and had settled her in.

'I'm bit tired,' Scarlet lied. 'I probably shouldn't have come in but I really wanted to finish up the placement.'

'Go home,' Beth said, and signed off her card. 'Do you have any questions?'

'No,' Scarlet said, when usually she had about a hundred and twenty of them. They could wait, her baby was refusing to. She really wanted to go and find Luke. 'I might go home actually, if that's okay.'

Beth nodded and Scarlet didn't bother to grab her bag, she just left the maternity unit to take the elevator to the ground floor, and as she got in there was Angie.

'Hi, Lucy Edwards.' Angie smiled.

It was a joke they shared now and then.

'Hi.' Scarlet smiled back.

'Where are you off to?'

'Coffee break,' Scarlet said. 'I am starving.'

She lied and Beth knew that she lied. The canteen wasn't that way!

But there were some things she didn't want to discuss with Angie, or Beth, or anyone else, except the man who was, Scarlet soon found out, elbow deep in something in Resus.

'Can you tell Luke I'm free for a coffee?' Scarlet said to Barbara, who was dashing back into Resus.

'He's a bit busy at the moment,' Barbara said, then she saw Scarlet's lips press together. 'I'll let him know you're here.'

Barbara went into Resus, where Luke was observing Sahin put in a chest drain. 'Scarlet's here,' Barbara said.

'Tell her to go for her break without me, I'm going to be a while.'

'Sure.' Barbara headed back outside. 'He said go ahead without him.' Barbara smiled.

'It's fine,' Scarlet said. 'I'll wait. I might go round to his office if that's okay?'

'Sure.' Barbara frowned and watched as Scarlet walked off.

At first Scarlet had been a bit of a shadow, coming down for lunch or coffee, but not lately, though.

She was tiny. From the back she didn't even look pregnant but then she stopped walking for long enough for Barbara to guess the real reason that Scarlet wanted to see Luke.

She went back into Resus. 'Scarlet said that she's going to wait in your office.'

'Fine.'

'Luke,' Barbara said, and Luke looked at her and into the eyes of a very experienced nurse.

'Yes?'

'I'm saying nothing,' Barbara said. 'Except that I think Sahin can take over from here.'

Sahin could. There was just the drain to be sutured in so

Sahin nodded and Luke stripped off his gown and gloves, washed his hands and headed through the department.

There were a few people staring. They'd seen Scarlet waddle around to his office and now a usually unruffled Luke was walking briskly.

He didn't stop to enlighten them!

Luke walked into his office and Scarlet stood there. As he had done many months ago, he saw her fear and turned on the engaged sign and never, ever would she take for granted the luxury of his arms and leaning against this chest and the bliss of the silence that he gave her when she needed it most.

Neither would Luke ever readily dismiss the scent of her hair and the knowledge that even as they stood still life was changing for ever.

Their baby kicked and Scarlet let go of the sob of fear that she'd been holding in for the last hour, just as Hannah had decided that she'd wanted Scarlet to stay close.

Luke felt her stomach tighten and his hand moved between them and he was surprised at the lack of noise from Scarlet because this was a long, deep contraction.

'How often are you getting them?'

'They're getting closer,' Scarlet said. 'I thought it took ages.'

'It might still,' Luke said, and he held her for a long moment but then changed his mind as she moaned into him and tried to bend at her knees. They weren't even two minutes apart!

'Do they know upstairs that you're in labour?' Luke checked.

'No.' Scarlet shook her head. Just as she had wanted to hear it from him if it had been bad news about her mother, she wanted to tell him when it was good.

'Isn't it too soon?'

She knew thirty-six weeks was a bit early but that the baby should be okay. However, she wanted to hear it from him.

'Scarlet, the baby will be just fine.'

He was always so calm.

'I'll call the labour ward and we can head up,' Luke suggested, reaching for the phone.

'I think I might need a chair.'

She had walked, almost run the whole way down to Emergency, holding her secret within her, but the thought of heading up that corridor now was daunting. Luke was, not that he'd show it, also feeling a bit daunted. Scarlet had her hands on his desk and her knees were bending again and she looked as if, at any second, she might squat.

'Barbara!' Luke buzzed around to the department and a few moments later Barbara came with a chair and a blanket.

'Can you call them again and tell them that I want an epidural?' Scarlet said rather urgently to Luke as she clung to the sides of the wheelchair, because it was starting to hurt seriously.

'I'll do that,' Barbara said, and shared a look with Luke. 'Maybe take Scarlet up now.'

'You will call ahead?' Scarlet checked, and thanked Barbara, who put the blanket over her knees.

It was the last time Scarlet remembered to be polite!

On the way to Maternity her waters broke and Scarlet had never been more grateful for the blanket, but by the time the lift got to Maternity she didn't even care about that any more.

'Scarlet!' Beth wasn't surprised to see her, Barbara had called ahead after all, but she was very surprised to see that Scarlet's toes were curling and that she was gripping the arms of the chair. 'Straight through,' Beth said.

'I want my epidural.'

'David's been held up,' Beth told her, rather than telling her that that they were way past that window.

'I don't want to hear it!'

Luke undressed her as Beth gave up trying to attach her to a monitor as Scarlet screamed out her demands.

'You will pull strings,' Scarlet demanded of Luke. 'You will call in favours...'

Scarlet was in full diva mode.

But today she was allowed to be.

'I'm not wearing that.' She just tossed the gown to the floor. 'Where's my epidural?'

'It's too late for that,' Beth soothed.

It didn't work.

'This is barbaric!' Scarlet screamed.

'I know, baby...' Luke too attempted to soothe her but he was quickly shot down.

'Don't tell me you know!'

'You're doing a fantastic job, Scarlet,' Beth said.

Oh, she was swaying, she was shouting, she was sucking on the green whistle, and she really was doing a fantastic job!

'I need to go to the restroom,' Scarlet begged.

'Scarlet,' Beth said patiently, 'you don't. That's your baby...'

And then Scarlet found out there was something she was very, very good at.

Pushing.

She just crouched down and grunted, and instinctively she knew what she needed to do.

'Okay...' David rushed in. 'I'm sorry it took so long to get here. Scarlet...?'

'Get out,' she shouted, and then got back to closing her eyes.

'I want to get on my knees,' she said.

'You can,' Beth said and massaged her back.

Luke knelt down and faced her.

'This is the worst…' Scarlet started to say, but then she stopped and they smiled because this was nowhere close to the worst. She looked right into his eyes and found herself lost there for the sweetest moment. She was exactly where she wanted to be. 'This is the best,' Scarlet said.

'You're the best,' Luke said, because staff were coming for a very rapid progression.

'Go, go, go…' Scarlet said to him, because her baby was coming, and Luke went around and out came a head. He watched it turn.

He saw the dark, cloudy hair and then two eyes opened and he knew even before she was out that he was a father to a little girl. Just as he acknowledged that fact, she was born into his hands.

He passed the baby up to her mother and she sat there, holding her and crying and kissing her little girl.

And there was another thing that Scarlet took easily to—breastfeeding.

She just sat on the cold floor and held and fed her little girl as the cord was cut and the placenta was delivered.

Even as they got her into bed, Scarlet could not let her go. They didn't have a name for her yet, so she was tagged Baby Edwards.

'I'm being selfish,' Scarlet said, because she knew she should let Luke hold her, but her naked skin was keeping the baby warm and Beth put a blanket over them.

'Be as selfish as you like,' Luke said.

He had made them wait for this moment. He had kept

that promise and even though they were rock solid he had
insisted that they did not rush into parenthood.

Scarlet had wanted a career, she had just wanted a stab
at the world, and he'd encouraged that. They'd celebrated
when she'd been accepted to study midwifery and their
lives had been happy and busy, but her want for a baby
had remained.

And now, finally, their daughter was here.

He watched as the baby stopped feeding.

'She's a bit small,' Beth said, 'so she'll tire quickly.'
Scarlet knew that she might need some top-up feeds and
she looked at the warmer waiting for their baby, who might
need a little bit of help too to regulate her temperature for
the next few days. Scarlet rested back on the pillow, looking down at their tiny baby, and then she handed their
daughter to Luke.

He lifted the tiny scrap that was lighter than he could
comprehend, and weighted his heart with happiness to
hold her.

She watched him look into his daughter's eyes and hold
her tiny fingers, and for the second time ever she saw tears
in his eyes.

They were happy ones now.

'She's beautiful.'

Absolutely she was. A shock of dark hair and navy eyes
that might stay the same colour or turn to chocolate brown,
and she had lips that were as perfect as Scarlet's now that
she'd given up on fillers.

He pulled back the blanket and looked at slender pink
feet and then wrapped them back up in the rug. Beth came
and put a little yellow hat on her and he knew soon he
would have to put her down.

'She's perfect,' Luke said. 'Like her mum.'

Scarlet was going to be an amazing mother, Luke knew,

and in turn he would give his daughter the childhood that her mother had never had.

They'd got this, Luke thought, and then he handed her back to Scarlet.

'She needs to go under the warmer,' Beth said. 'Don't worry, she can stay beside you.' They watched as she slept and her perfect little mouth slipped into what looked like a sleepy smile as Beth got on with the paperwork.

'Have you thought of a name?' Beth checked.

Scarlet looked at Luke and he nodded.

'Emily,' Scarlet said. 'Emily Edwards.'

There would be a couple of hooks at school with the same name, no doubt, and that suited them both just fine.

'I'm starving,' Scarlet said, as, on the maternity ward, she climbed into bed and Beth plugged in the warmer so that Emily could stay with them.

Scarlet had walked round to the ward, rather than be wheeled there. Had he not seen her just give birth, he wouldn't have known she had.

Every day she surprised Luke more and more. Scarlet was so much tougher than she looked.

'I'm seriously starving,' Scarlet said, and looked at Luke. 'Can you get me a muffin?'

They were her favourite thing from the vending machine.

'You've earned more than a muffin,' Beth said. 'It's a bit early for the lunches to come round so I'll go and see if there are any breakfasts left.'

There were.

Toast, scrambled eggs, bacon and mushrooms.

No grapefruit juice, though.

Scarlet pouted.

'It's still pretty perfect,' Luke said, and got up on the bed by her side.

Oh, it was.
Breakfast in bed, with their baby by their side.
It was a very good morning.
They all were now!

* * * * *

MILLS & BOON®
Hardback – March 2016

ROMANCE

The Italian's Ruthless Seduction	Miranda Lee
Awakened by Her Desert Captor	Abby Green
A Forbidden Temptation	Anne Mather
A Vow to Secure His Legacy	Annie West
Carrying the King's Pride	Jennifer Hayward
Bound to the Tuscan Billionaire	Susan Stephens
Required to Wear the Tycoon's Ring	Maggie Cox
The Secret That Shocked De Santis	Natalie Anderson
The Greek's Ready-Made Wife	Jennifer Faye
Crown Prince's Chosen Bride	Kandy Shepherd
Billionaire, Boss...Bridegroom?	Kate Hardy
Married for their Miracle Baby	Soraya Lane
The Socialite's Secret	Carol Marinelli
London's Most Eligible Doctor	Annie O'Neil
Saving Maddie's Baby	Marion Lennox
A Sheikh to Capture Her Heart	Meredith Webber
Breaking All Their Rules	Sue MacKay
One Life-Changing Night	Louisa Heaton
The CEO's Unexpected Child	Andrea Laurence
Snowbound with the Boss	Maureen Child

MILLS & BOON®
Large Print – March 2016

ROMANCE

A Christmas Vow of Seduction	Maisey Yates
Brazilian's Nine Months' Notice	Susan Stephens
The Sheikh's Christmas Conquest	Sharon Kendrick
Shackled to the Sheikh	Trish Morey
Unwrapping the Castelli Secret	Caitlin Crews
A Marriage Fit for a Sinner	Maya Blake
Larenzo's Christmas Baby	Kate Hewitt
His Lost-and-Found Bride	Scarlet Wilson
Housekeeper Under the Mistletoe	Cara Colter
Gift-Wrapped in Her Wedding Dress	Kandy Shepherd
The Prince's Christmas Vow	Jennifer Faye

HISTORICAL

His Housekeeper's Christmas Wish	Louise Allen
Temptation of a Governess	Sarah Mallory
The Demure Miss Manning	Amanda McCabe
Enticing Benedict Cole	Eliza Redgold
In the King's Service	Margaret Moore

MEDICAL

Falling at the Surgeon's Feet	Lucy Ryder
One Night in New York	Amy Ruttan
Daredevil, Doctor...Husband?	Alison Roberts
The Doctor She'd Never Forget	Annie Claydon
Reunited...in Paris!	Sue MacKay
French Fling to Forever	Karin Baine

MILLS & BOON®
Hardback – April 2016

ROMANCE

The Sicilian's Stolen Son	Lynne Graham
Seduced into Her Boss's Service	Cathy Williams
The Billionaire's Defiant Acquisition	Sharon Kendrick
One Night to Wedding Vows	Kim Lawrence
Engaged to Her Ravensdale Enemy	Melanie Milburne
A Diamond Deal with the Greek	Maya Blake
Inherited by Ferranti	Kate Hewitt
The Secret to Marrying Marchesi	Amanda Cinelli
The Billionaire's Baby Swap	Rebecca Winters
The Wedding Planner's Big Day	Cara Colter
Holiday with the Best Man	Kate Hardy
Tempted by Her Tycoon Boss	Jennie Adams
Seduced by the Heart Surgeon	Carol Marinelli
Falling for the Single Dad	Emily Forbes
The Fling That Changed Everything	Alison Roberts
A Child to Open Their Hearts	Marion Lennox
The Greek Doctor's Secret Son	Jennifer Taylor
Caught in a Storm of Passion	Lucy Ryder
Take Me, Cowboy	Maisey Yates
His Baby Agenda	Katherine Garbera

MILLS & BOON®
Large Print – April 2016

ROMANCE

The Price of His Redemption	Carol Marinelli
Back in the Brazilian's Bed	Susan Stephens
The Innocent's Sinful Craving	Sara Craven
Brunetti's Secret Son	Maya Blake
Talos Claims His Virgin	Michelle Smart
Destined for the Desert King	Kate Walker
Ravensdale's Defiant Captive	Melanie Milburne
The Best Man & The Wedding Planner	Teresa Carpenter
Proposal at the Winter Ball	Jessica Gilmore
Bodyguard...to Bridegroom?	Nikki Logan
Christmas Kisses with Her Boss	Nina Milne

HISTORICAL

His Christmas Countess	Louise Allen
The Captain's Christmas Bride	Annie Burrows
Lord Lansbury's Christmas Wedding	Helen Dickson
Warrior of Fire	Michelle Willingham
Lady Rowena's Ruin	Carol Townend

MEDICAL

The Baby of Their Dreams	Carol Marinelli
Falling for Her Reluctant Sheikh	Amalie Berlin
Hot-Shot Doc, Secret Dad	Lynne Marshall
Father for Her Newborn Baby	Lynne Marshall
His Little Christmas Miracle	Emily Forbes
Safe in the Surgeon's Arms	Molly Evans

MILLS & BOON®

Why shop at millsandboon.co.uk?

Each year, thousands of romance readers find their perfect read at millsandboon.co.uk. That's because we're passionate about bringing you the very best romantic fiction. Here are some of the advantages of shopping at www.millsandboon.co.uk:

* **Get new books first**—you'll be able to buy your favourite books one month before they hit the shops

* **Get exclusive discounts**—you'll also be able to buy our specially created monthly collections, with up to 50% off the RRP

* **Find your favourite authors**—latest news, interviews and new releases for all your favourite authors and series on our website, plus ideas for what to try next

* **Join in**—once you've bought your favourite books, don't forget to register with us to rate, review and join in the discussions

Visit **www.millsandboon.co.uk**
for all this and more today!